ELENA ROSEWOOD

A Lady's Indecent Season

A Regency Erotica

First edition

This book was professionally typeset on Reedsy.
Find out more at reedsy.com

Contents

Prologue

The drawing room of Featherington House vibrated with the nervous energy of its newest resident as Lady Cecilia Featherington stood rigid while her lady's maid, Betty, yanked mercilessly at her corset strings.

"Tighter, Betty. Mother insists my waist must not exceed seventeen inches for my debut." Cecilia gripped the bedpost, her knuckles white.

"Begging your pardon, m'lady, but you'll faint dead away before the first dance if I pull any harder," Betty warned, her face reddening with exertion.

"Nonsense. The art of attracting a husband apparently requires the systematic restriction of one's internal organs." Cecilia rolled her eyes when Betty wasn't looking. "One must suffer for the pleasure of being paraded like a prize heifer at Smithfield Market."

Though if the gentlemen are as dull as Lord Thistlewhite, who visited yesterday, I'd rather remain on the shelf indefinitely, Cecilia thought, wincing as Betty secured the laces.

The bedroom door flew open without warning, and Lady Agatha Featherington swept in, a vision of maternal anxiety adorned with an inexplicable quantity of ostrich feathers.

"Cecilia! We depart for Almack's in one hour, and you're still half-dressed! The vouchers weren't easy to secure, I'll have you know. I had to compliment Lady Jersey's new turban, which looked precisely like a diseased peacock perched atop her head." She fluttered around the room, a nervous bird in expensive silk. "The Duke of Greystone is rumored to be in attendance tonight."

Cecilia sighed. "Another dissipated nobleman with more titles than teeth, I presume?"

Lady Agatha gasped, her hand flying to her throat dramatically. "You will guard that impertinent tongue, daughter! The Duke is one of England's most eligible bachelors, despite his... reputation."

"What reputation?" Cecilia asked, suddenly interested.

"Never you mind!" Lady Agatha snapped. "Just ensure you appear suitably virginal and witless. Men of his station prefer their wives decorative and silent."

After her mother swept out in another flurry of feathers, Cecilia submitted to being stuffed into her debut gown—a confection of ivory silk with puffed sleeves so enormous she feared she might achieve flight if she moved too quickly.

"You look beautiful, m'lady," Betty said, securing the final of twenty-three pearl buttons that marched up Cecilia's back.

"I look like a meringue with eyes," Cecilia muttered, surveying herself in the mirror. The gown's modesty was laughable— while her décolletage was barely visible, the thin silk clung to her corseted waist and rounded hips in a way that somehow seemed more indecent than if she'd worn nothing at all.

At least the color doesn't make me look consumptive, she thought, pinching her cheeks to bring color to them. *Small mercies.*

Hours later, Cecilia found herself pressed against the wall of Almack's hallowed assembly rooms, desperately seeking a moment's respite from the endless introductions to gentlemen whose names and faces blurred together in a parade of pomaded hair and predatory smiles.

"If one more man comments on the 'fine weather we're having' while staring at my bosom, I may commit an act of violence involving a punch ladle," she muttered to herself, slipping away from the ballroom and down a corridor.

A door stood ajar, golden lamplight spilling invitingly into the hallway. Cecilia glanced over her shoulder and, seeing no one, slipped inside what appeared to be a small library.

"Thank goodness," she breathed, running her fingers along the leather-bound spines. Books, at least, made reliable companions.

"Are you searching for anything in particular?" a deep voice inquired from behind her.

Cecilia yelped, spinning around so quickly her ridiculous sleeves nearly knocked over a small bust of Aristotle. A man lounged in a leather chair partially hidden by a bookcase— tall, broad-shouldered, with tousled dark hair and the most wickedly amused blue eyes she'd ever encountered.

"Forgive me," she stammered. "I didn't realize the room was occupied."

"Clearly." His mouth curved into a smile that transformed his austere features into something dangerously appealing. "Most debutantes search for husbands in the ballroom, not the library."

"Perhaps that explains why so many end up disappointed in their matches," Cecilia replied before she could stop herself.

Instead of offense, his smile widened to reveal perfect white teeth. "An excellent point. The character of a potential spouse might indeed be better judged by their reading material than their quadrille."

He uncurled from the chair with the languid grace of a predator and approached her. Cecilia should have retreated— a proper lady would never remain unchaperoned with an unknown gentleman—but curiosity rooted her to the spot.

"Sebastian Blackwood," he said with a slight bow. "Duke of Greystone, though I prefer to avoid the tedious formalities when possible."

The Duke of Greystone! Cecilia's heart hammered against her ribs. The gossip pages called him the "Duke of Debauchery" for his rumored sexual appetites and collection of erotic art from the continent.

"Lady Cecilia Featherington," she replied with a curtsy so low her preposterous sleeves brushed the carpet.

"Lady Cecilia," he repeated, his voice caressing her name in a manner that seemed indecent. "A saint's name, isn't it? Yet I suspect there's precious little saintly about you."

Heat flooded her cheeks. "You presume much, Your Grace, having known me but two minutes."

"Do I?" He stepped closer. "Then explain why a properly raised young lady seeks solitude in a gentleman's library rather than matrimonial prospects on the dance floor."

"Perhaps I find books more stimulating than conversation about the weather," she replied, lifting her chin defiantly.

"Indeed." His eyes sparkled with mischief. "Then allow me to recommend something truly... stimulating."

He reached past her—so close she could smell sandalwood and brandy on his skin—and pulled a slim volume from a high shelf, his arm brushing against hers in a touch that, while brief, sent a shocking thrill through her body.

"This might appeal to your... intellectual curiosity," he murmured, placing the book in her hands.

Cecilia glanced down and nearly dropped the volume when she realized what she was holding. The leather cover bore no title, but the book fell open to an engraving so explicitly carnal she couldn't comprehend it for several seconds. A man and woman entwined in a position that defied both gravity and Cecilia's understanding of human anatomy.

"This is—" she sputtered, unable to tear her eyes away from the image.

"French," he supplied helpfully. "The artist has a particularly vivid imagination, though I can assure you the position is entirely possible with sufficient flexibility and motivation."

Cecilia knew she should be outraged, should slap his face and flee the room with her virtue and reputation intact. Instead, she found herself tilting her head slightly, reassessing the engraving from a different angle.

"The lady would need exceptional balance," she observed clinically, surprising even herself.

The Duke's laugh was rich and genuine. "And the gentleman, considerable stamina." His fingers brushed hers as he reclaimed the book, the brief contact sending another jolt through her. "You're not at all what I expected, Lady Cecilia."

"Nor you, Your Grace." She met his gaze boldly. "I was warned you were dangerous."

"Oh, I am." His voice dropped to a velvet rumble. "Particularly to young ladies who prefer French erotica to marriage-minded quadrilles."

Before she could formulate a suitably witty response, the

library door swung open, and Lady Agatha's voice shattered the moment.

"Cecilia! I've been searching everywhere—" Her mother froze, taking in the scene with mounting horror: her daughter, alone with the notorious Duke, standing entirely too close to be proper. "Your Grace! I... we... that is to say..."

The Duke stepped smoothly away from Cecilia, bowing formally to Lady Agatha. "Lady Featherington. I was just assisting your daughter in reaching a historical tome she expressed interest in."

"A history of French architecture," Cecilia improvised wildly, gesturing vaguely at the bookshelves.

"How... educational," Lady Agatha managed, her eyes darting suspiciously between them. "However, Lord Thistlewhite awaits your presence for the next dance, Cecilia."

"Don't let me keep you from such a thrilling prospect," the Duke said with a perfectly straight face, though his eyes gleamed with amusement. "Though perhaps we might continue our discussion of... architecture... at Lady Melbourne's rout tomorrow?"

"Lady Cecilia's dance card is quite full for the foreseeable future," Lady Agatha interjected, seizing her daughter's arm.

As her mother practically dragged her from the library, Cecilia glanced back over her shoulder. The Duke watched her departure with an expression of such deliberate, promised wickedness that her stays suddenly felt twice as tight.

This Season might not be as dreadful as I feared, she thought, a smile tugging at her lips as Lady Agatha marched her back toward the unsuspecting Lord Thistlewhite and his weak chin.

Behind them, the Duke's soft laughter lingered in the corridor like a promise.

Chapter 1

Lady Cecilia Featherington was not hiding.

Hiding would be childish, and at two-and-twenty, she was most certainly not a child. She was merely... strategically relocating herself within the elaborate hedge maze at Lady Hartwick's garden party, specifically to a location where Lord Percival Thistlewhite and his wandering, clammy hands could not find her.

"If he compares my eyes to 'dewy moonbeams' one more time, I cannot be held responsible for my actions," she muttered, lifting her skirts to navigate a particularly narrow passage between towering yew hedges. Her fashionable walking dress—a pale yellow muslin adorned with approximately seventeen thousand tiny embroidered daisies—snagged on the foliage with every step, as if the garment itself were conspiring to reveal her location.

The sound of approaching voices sent her darting around a corner, where she collided with something solid, warm, and distinctly male.

"Lady Cecilia," drawled a now-familiar voice. "How remarkable to find you lurking in the shrubbery. One might almost suspect you were avoiding someone."

Sebastian Blackwood, the Duke of Greystone, steadied her with hands that lingered perhaps a moment longer than strictly necessary on her waist. In the week since their encounter in the library, Cecilia had spotted him at three different social events, each time exchanging glances charged with something unspoken that left her feeling both unsettled and exhilarated.

"Your Grace." She dropped into a curtsy that she immediately recognized as too deep for a casual garden meeting, revealing her flustered state. "I was simply enjoying a solitary constitutional."

"In a maze designed specifically to cause confusion and distress?" His eyes crinkled with amusement. "How adventurous."

"Less distressing than Lord Thistlewhite's poetry," she replied before she could stop herself.

The Duke threw back his head and laughed, the sound sending an inappropriate thrill through her. He looked absurdly handsome in his informal attire—buckskin breeches that clung indecently to his muscular thighs, a blue coat that emphasized the breadth of his shoulders, and a cravat tied in a style so complex it seemed to defy the laws of physics.

"Poor Thistlewhite. The man has the literary talent of a concussed goose." His smile turned predatory as he stepped closer. "I must confess, I've been seeking a private audience with you all week."

"Have you indeed?" Cecilia lifted her chin, affecting a nonchalance she didn't feel as her pulse quickened. "How persistent of you."

"You've proven remarkably elusive for a debutante. Almost

as if your mother has been deliberately keeping you from my corrupting influence."

"Mother believes you harbor dishonorable intentions."

"Your mother," he said, moving closer still, "is entirely correct."

Cecilia swallowed hard, suddenly acutely aware of how alone they were in this secluded corner of the maze. The distant sounds of the garden party seemed to belong to another world entirely.

"Is that your infamous indecent proposal, then?" she asked, proud that her voice remained steady.

"Merely a statement of fact." He reached out, boldly tucking a stray curl behind her ear. "My intentions toward you are spectacularly dishonorable. I've thought of little else since finding you with that book of French erotica."

"You placed it in my hands," she reminded him, not stepping away as propriety demanded.

"And you didn't immediately drop it in horror." His fingers traced the line of her jaw. "Which suggests you might be receptive to an arrangement of mutual... educational value."

I should be scandalized, Cecilia thought. *I should slap his face and storm away in righteous indignation.* Instead, she found herself leaning subtly into his touch, curiosity and desire overwhelming years of proper instruction.

"What sort of arrangement?" The words emerged as barely more than a whisper.

The Duke's eyes darkened. "The sort where I introduce you to pleasures your mother would never include in your deportment lessons."

"How remarkably presumptuous of you." Despite her words, Cecilia made no move to leave. "What makes you think I'd risk my reputation for such an arrangement?"

"The fact that you're still standing here, entertaining this conversation." His thumb brushed her lower lip, sending a shock of sensation straight to parts of her anatomy that had never featured in her mother's discussions of proper ladylike behavior. "The way your breath quickens when I stand close to you. The fact that you've just moistened your lips while staring at mine."

Cecilia hadn't realized she'd done so until he mentioned it. "Perhaps I'm simply gathering evidence of your scandalous behavior to report to the patronesses of Almack's."

"Then by all means, gather more evidence."

He closed the remaining distance between them and claimed her mouth with his. The shock of the contact froze Cecilia momentarily—her first kiss, delivered by a duke in a hedge maze, without a proper offer of marriage or even an understanding between them. It was outrageous, improper, and utterly thrilling.

His lips were warm and surprisingly soft, moving against hers with practiced skill. Just as Cecilia began to respond, her hands creeping up to touch his impossibly starched cravat, he broke the kiss, leaving her swaying slightly and struggling to remember why this was such a terrible idea.

"That," he murmured, "was merely a preview of my educational curriculum."

"Quite… instructive," she managed, her voice embarrassingly breathy.

"I haven't even begun to teach you, Lady Cecilia." The wicked promise in his voice made her knees weaken. "Though I suspect you'll be an exceptionally quick study."

The sound of someone calling her name penetrated their

10

private bubble. Lord Thistlewhite's nasal voice echoed through the maze, coming closer.

"Damnation," the Duke muttered. "Your admirer approaches."

"He's not my admirer, he's my mother's choice," Cecilia corrected, gathering her scattered wits. "She believes his estate's proximity to our country home makes him ideal husband material, despite the fact that his conversation would bore a fence post to tears."

The Duke's expression darkened momentarily. "Meet me here, after the musical entertainment begins," he said, his voice low and urgent. "Everyone will be trapped listening to Lady Hartwick's daughters massacre Mozart for at least an hour."

Cecilia knew she should refuse. Meeting a man—especially this man—alone and unchaperoned was precisely the sort of behavior that ruined young ladies. And yet...

"I make no promises," she said primly, even as her mind had already decided.

"Lady Cecilia! There you are!" Lord Thistlewhite's voice called from alarmingly nearby. "I've composed a new verse comparing your complexion to freshly churned butter!"

The Duke raised an eyebrow. "Freshly churned butter?"

"The height of romance, clearly," Cecilia whispered sarcastically.

"I'll wait by the stone bench at the center," the Duke murmured, then swiftly disappeared around a hedge just as Lord Thistlewhite rounded the corner, his tall collar so starched it appeared to be slowly strangling him.

"Lady Cecilia! I feared you were lost in this dreadful maze," he exclaimed, his prominent Adam's apple bobbing with emotion. "Your mother has been searching for you."

Of course she has, Cecilia thought grimly. *Heaven forbid I enjoy five minutes without supervision.*

"How fortunate you found me, then," she replied with a smile so false it made her cheeks ache. "Shall we return to the party?"

* * *

As Lady Hartwick's youngest daughter murdered a sonata with enthusiastic incompetence, Cecilia slipped away from the gathered guests with practiced stealth. Her mother, mercifully occupied with critiquing Lady Jersey's latest turban innovation, didn't notice her departure.

The sun had begun its descent, casting long shadows across the garden as Cecilia found her way back into the maze, heart pounding with a mixture of trepidation and exhilaration. The sensible part of her brain—which sounded suspiciously like her mother—screamed warnings about ruination and scandal.

The far less sensible part—which had been growing steadily louder since meeting the Duke—whispered that life without adventure was hardly worth living at all.

She found him exactly where he'd promised, lounging on the stone bench at the center of the maze like a pagan god entertaining himself among mortals. He rose when he saw her, genuine surprise flashing briefly across his features.

"You came," he said, sounding both pleased and impressed.

"Apparently, I've taken leave of my senses," Cecilia replied, remaining at what she deemed a safe distance. "I should warn you that if you're planning to compromise me to force a marriage, I have virtually no dowry to recommend me, and my mother snores loudly enough to wake the dead."

The Duke burst out laughing. "What a mercenary you believe me to be. I have no need of your non-existent dowry, and I've already suffered through one overbearing mother—I've no wish to acquire another." He patted the bench beside him. "Won't you sit? I promise not to bite. Unless specifically requested."

Cecilia hesitated, then sat, carefully arranging her skirts and leaving what she considered an appropriate distance between them. "Why me? Surely there are dozens of willing widows who would happily enter into your 'arrangement' without the complications of innocence."

"Precisely because you're not like the others." He turned to face her, his expression surprisingly earnest. "You hide a sharp mind behind those proper manners, and you look at those French engravings with curiosity rather than shock. You intrigue me, Lady Cecilia."

"That's hardly a compelling reason to risk my reputation."

"Perhaps not." He shifted closer. "Then allow me to offer a more compelling one."

This time when he kissed her, Cecilia was prepared—or so she thought. But the gentle press of his lips from their first encounter transformed into something far more demanding. His mouth moved against hers with a hunger that awakened an answering need within her. When his tongue traced the seam of her lips, she gasped in surprise, inadvertently allowing him access.

Oh my, she thought dizzily as his tongue slid against hers, teaching her a dance far more intimate than anything performed in Almack's. *No one mentioned this part.*

His hand came up to cradle her face, tilting her head to deepen the kiss as his other arm wrapped around her waist, drawing her closer. Cecilia found herself responding instinctively, her hands clutching the lapels of his perfectly tailored coat as heat bloomed low in her belly.

When they finally broke apart, she was practically in his lap, one of her ridiculous daisy-embroidered sleeves partially detached and hanging limply from her shoulder.

"That," she said breathlessly, "was definitely more compelling."

The Duke's eyes had darkened to midnight, his breathing as uneven as hers. "That was merely the introduction to our first lesson."

His hand slid up her arm to the loosened sleeve, his fingers brushing against the exposed skin of her shoulder. "May I continue your education, Lady Cecilia?"

Every lesson she'd ever received about propriety and virtue screamed at her to stop this madness immediately. And yet…

"Yes," she whispered, surprising herself with her boldness. "Though I believe I mentioned I prefer to be called just Cecilia."

"And I prefer Sebastian," he replied, his fingers finding the row of tiny pearl buttons that marched down her back. "Particularly when moaned in ecstasy."

His deft fingers began unfastening her buttons with remarkable skill, each one releasing with a tiny pop that seemed obscenely loud in the quiet of the maze. "How many blasted buttons does this gown have?" he muttered against her neck, where his lips had begun tracing a scorching path.

"Twenty-three," Cecilia gasped as his teeth grazed a particularly sensitive spot below her ear. "Betty counts them every morning while dressing me."

"Remind me to have words with your dressmaker about this excessive barricade," Sebastian growled, his fingers continuing their patient work. "Though there is something to be said for the anticipation of unwrapping such an elaborate package."

With each button he released, Cecilia felt not only her gown loosening but also her lifelong constraints falling away. By the fifteenth button, the bodice had grown slack enough that he could ease it forward over her shoulders, exposing her chemise and the swell of her breasts above her corset.

"Beautiful," he murmured, his gaze hot as it traveled over her partially exposed form. "Though these underpinnings appear to be another defense system entirely."

Cecilia laughed shakily. "Mother says a proper lady's under-garments should be as impenetrable as her virtue."

"Your mother underestimates my determination." Sebastian's hands slid up to cup her breasts through the thin fabric of her chemise, his thumbs brushing over the peaks that had hardened traitorously at his touch. Even through layers of fabric, the sensation pulled a startled moan from her throat.

"Sensitive," he observed with a wicked smile, repeating the motion and watching her reaction with fascination. "I wonder how you'll respond when there's nothing between my mouth and these perfect nipples."

The crude language should have shocked her. Instead, it sent a surge of liquid heat between her thighs. "You shouldn't say such things," she admonished halfheartedly.

"You shouldn't enjoy them so visibly," he countered, lowering his head to press his open mouth against the upper swell of her breast, his hot breath penetrating the thin chemise.

Cecilia's head fell back as sensation overwhelmed her. His hands seemed to be everywhere—skimming her sides, cupping her breasts, traveling boldly up her stockinged leg beneath her skirts. When his fingers encountered the ribbon of her garter, she jolted in surprise.

"Perhaps we should continue this educational experience somewhere more private," Sebastian suggested, his voice strained as he reluctantly withdrew his hand. "As much as I enjoy the thought of taking you right here where anyone might discover us, your first time deserves a bed, at minimum."

Cecilia blinked, reality crashing back. "My first... Oh!" She scrambled to pull her bodice back up, suddenly aware of how disheveled she must look. "We can't possibly—that is to say—I never meant to imply—"

Sebastian caught her fluttering hands in his. "Breathe, Cecilia. I'm not suggesting we complete the act here and now." His smile turned predatory. "Though I am suggesting we continue at the earliest opportunity. Perhaps during Lady Melbourne's masked ball tomorrow night? The terrace gardens have several secluded pavilions ideal for private... conversations."

The sound of voices drifted toward them—the musical portion of the entertainment had apparently concluded, and guests were returning to the gardens. Cecilia hurriedly tried to refasten her buttons, but the awkward angle made it impossible.

"Allow me," Sebastian said, turning her gently. His fingers worked with surprising efficiency, securing her back into re-spectability. "Though it seems a shame to cover such loveliness."

Just as he fastened the final button, Lady Agatha's voice rang out, entirely too close for comfort. "Cecilia! Where have you gotten to, girl?"

"Perfect timing," Sebastian murmured, pressing a swift kiss to Cecilia's now properly covered shoulder. "Lady Melbourne's ball, tomorrow night. The Greek pavilion at the south end of the terrace, eleven o'clock." He stepped back, smoothing his own somewhat rumpled appearance. "I'll depart first and create a diversion. Wait five minutes, then follow the path to the left."

Before she could respond, he was gone, leaving Cecilia alone on the bench, her lips swollen from his kisses and her body humming with unfulfilled desire.

What am I doing? she wondered, attempting to tidy her hopelessly mussed hair. *This is madness. Utter madness.*

And yet, as she smoothed her skirts and prepared to face her mother with what she hoped was an innocent expression, she knew with absolute certainty that tomorrow night at eleven o'clock, she would be at the Greek pavilion, propriety and good sense be damned.

Behind her, Sebastian's voice carried clearly across the garden, greeting Lady Agatha with excessive enthusiasm. "Lady Featherington! I've been searching everywhere for you. I simply must know where you acquired that magnificent headdress. Is that an entire stuffed pheasant, or merely its plumage?"

Cecilia bit her lip to stifle her laughter and slipped away in the opposite direction, already counting the hours until tomorrow night.

Chapter 2

Lady Melbourne's annual masked ball was the crown jewel of the Season, an event so exclusive that matrons had been known to resort to bribery, blackmail, and in one notorious instance involving the Countess of Lipton, a trained ferret, to secure invitations. The ballroom glittered with hundreds of candles, gilt mirrors multiplying their light until the space seemed enchanted. Through her silver filigree mask, Cecilia surveyed the crowd, attempting to appear interested in Lord Thistlewhite's dissertation on turnip cultivation while her mind fixated on the approaching hour of eleven.

"The secret, you see, is in the rotation of the fields," Thistlewhite droned, his Adam's apple bobbing above his excessively starched collar. "My tenants were skeptical at first, but when they saw the size of my turnips—"

"Fascinating," Cecilia interrupted, having reached her limit on root vegetable discourse. "Would you be so kind as to fetch me some punch, Lord Thistlewhite? I find myself quite parched."

"Of course, Lady Cecilia!" He practically bowed in half, his eagerness to please painfully evident. "I shall return forthwith with the finest punch Lady Melbourne has to offer."

As he scurried away, Cecilia checked the ornate clock on the wall. Ten forty-five. Her stomach performed a complicated acrobatic maneuver that would have impressed the most seasoned circus performer.

This is madness, her rational mind insisted. *You cannot seriously be considering a midnight assignation with the most notorious rake in London.*

Watch me, replied the increasingly vocal rebellious part of her brain.

"Lady Cecilia." The deep voice behind her sent a shiver down her spine before she even turned.

Sebastian stood there, resplendent in formal black and white, his half-mask doing nothing to disguise his identity to anyone who had spent an embarrassing amount of time studying his features. His cravat seemed even more complicated than usual, an architectural marvel of starched white linen that would require substantial unwinding.

Stop thinking about unwinding his cravat, she scolded herself, dropping into a curtsy. "Your Grace."

"I couldn't help noticing Lord Thistlewhite monopolizing your attention," he said, his voice pitched for her ears alone. "Another poetry recitation?"

"Worse. Turnips."

Sebastian's laugh drew several curious glances. "The poor man has no idea how to properly engage a woman's interest."

"Unlike yourself?" Cecilia arched an eyebrow, surprising herself with her boldness.

"I believe I've demonstrated some skill in that area," he replied, eyes darkening behind his mask. "Though I'm eager to further prove my abilities." He glanced at the clock. "Perhaps we might practice a dance not commonly performed in English ballrooms?"

Cecilia felt heat rising in her cheeks. "I believe I would need private instruction for such a dance."

"As it happens, I am an excellent instructor." Sebastian offered his arm. "The music room should be available, as Lady Melbourne's daughters are all married and the pianoforte sees little use these days."

Every rule of propriety demanded Cecilia refuse, remind him of Lord Thistlewhite's imminent return with punch, and remain firmly in the crowded ballroom. Instead, she placed her gloved hand on his sleeve.

"Lead on, Professor," she murmured, her heart racing as he guided her toward the door.

They moved casually through the crowd, Sebastian nodding to acquaintances as they passed, maintaining a picture of perfect innocence. Only when they slipped into the deserted corridor did his demeanor change, his hand moving to the small of her back, guiding her with more intimate pressure.

"Third door on the left," he murmured, his breath warm against her ear. "Quick, before anyone notices."

The music room was dark save for moonlight streaming through tall windows. Sebastian closed the door behind them, the soft click of the latch unnervingly final.

I can still leave, Cecilia thought, even as she removed her mask and placed it on a side table. *Nothing has happened yet.*

"Second thoughts?" Sebastian asked, removing his own mask and studying her with those piercing blue eyes.

"At least a dozen," she admitted honestly. "Yet here I remain."

"Here you remain," he agreed, moving closer, the moonlight

casting half his face in shadow. "Alone with the man your mother has specifically warned you against."

"Mother also warned me against eating strawberries before dinner, claiming they would curdle in my stomach and cause dropsy," Cecilia replied. "Her medical knowledge is as suspect as her judgment of character."

Sebastian laughed, closing the distance between them. "I'm beginning to think I'm not nearly as much of a corrupter as I believed. You seem perfectly capable of corrupting yourself."

"Perhaps I simply needed the right accomplice." She surprised herself with her daring.

"Well then," he murmured, his hands settling on her waist. "Shall we begin your dance lesson, my lady?"

Without waiting for her response, his mouth captured hers in a kiss that made their previous encounters seem like mere practice. This kiss held nothing back—it was hot, demanding, and thoroughly indecent, his tongue plundering her mouth as his hands splayed across her back, pressing her against him until she could feel every hard plane of his body through the layers of their clothing.

Cecilia melted into him, her own hands clutching at his shoulders as she attempted to give as good as she got, mimicking the movements of his tongue with growing confidence. When his teeth gently caught her lower lip, she gasped, the unexpected spark of sensation shooting straight to her core.

"Quick study indeed," Sebastian breathed, his mouth trailing down her neck. "Now, for our first dance position..."

His hands slid confidently behind her, finding the row of buttons on her ball gown with practiced ease. Unlike her walking dress, tonight's creation—a confection of midnight blue silk trimmed with silver embroidery—featured only fifteen buttons, each concealed beneath a decorative silk bow.

"Your dressmaker believes in making me work for my reward," Sebastian murmured against her collarbone as his fingers dispatched the fastenings with remarkable dexterity.

"I believe she's more concerned with fashion than accessibility," Cecilia replied, her voice embarrassingly breathy as his knuckles brushed against her bare skin with each button he released.

"A critical oversight." The final button surrendered, and Sebastian eased the bodice forward. "For a garment should be as pleasing to remove as it is to look upon."

The gown slipped down to pool at her feet in a whisper of expensive silk, leaving Cecilia in her corset, chemise, petticoats, and stockings. She fought the urge to cover herself as Sebastian stepped back, his gaze traveling slowly over her partially dressed form with unconcealed appreciation.

"Beautiful," he said simply, his voice roughened with desire. "Though I fear we've reached another barricade." He circled behind her, fingers tracing the laces of her corset. "This contraption appears to require a team of engineers to dismantle."

Cecilia laughed despite her nervousness. "Betty employs a wooden dowel to achieve the necessary leverage."

"How resourceful." His breath was warm against her shoulder as he worked at the knot securing her laces. "Though I prefer a more... hands-on approach."

The laces loosened gradually under his persistent efforts, each incremental release allowing Cecilia to breathe a little deeper. When the corset finally gaped open, Sebastian slid it forward over her arms and tossed it unceremoniously atop her discarded gown.

"Better?" he asked, his hands settling on her waist, now

protected only by the thin linen of her chemise.

"Much," she admitted, reveling in the simple pleasure of unrestricted breathing. "Though I believe you're overdressed for this particular dance, sir."

Sebastian's eyebrows rose in surprise and delight at her boldness. "An excellent observation. Perhaps you'd care to assist with my attire?"

Cecilia stepped forward, her fingers trembling slightly as she reached for his elaborately tied cravat. "I should warn you that I have approximately no experience in undressing gentlemen."

"The theory is simple enough—it's merely the reverse of dressing." His hands covered hers, guiding her fingers to the first fold. "Begin here, and unwind counterclockwise."

The process of dismantling the architectural wonder of his cravat proved unexpectedly intimate. With each layer she unwound, Cecilia felt as though she were peeling away the public persona of the Duke of Greystone to reveal Sebastian the man. When the length of starched linen finally came free, his throat was exposed—a vulnerable hollow that she found herself wanting to taste.

Following her instincts, she rose on tiptoe and pressed her lips to the pulse point beneath his jaw. Sebastian sucked in a sharp breath, his hands tightening on her waist.

"You're a dangerously quick study," he growled, tilting his head to give her better access. "Continue with my waistcoat, if you please."

The waistcoat presented a new challenge—twelve small pearl buttons that required more dexterity than Cecilia's increasingly clumsy fingers possessed. After fumbling with the third button, Sebastian captured her hands.

"Perhaps we should advance the lesson," he suggested, making short work of the remaining buttons himself and shrugging out of both coat and waistcoat in one fluid movement. His fine lawn shirt clung to his broad shoulders, offering tantalizing hints of the muscled form beneath.

"Now," he said, leading her backward until she felt the edge of the pianoforte against her petticoats, "for the most interesting part of our continental dance."

In one smooth motion, he lifted her to sit on the closed keyboard cover, the unexpected movement drawing a surprised squeak from her throat. Before she could protest, he stepped between her knees, his hands pushing her petticoats upward to expose her stockinged legs.

"Sebastian!" she gasped, scandalized despite her willingness thus far.

"Learning a new dance requires surrendering to unfamiliar movements," he murmured, his hands sliding up her thighs to the ribbons securing her garters. "Do you trust me to lead, Cecilia?"

The use of her given name, combined with the hypnotic circles his thumbs were tracing against her inner thighs, made rational thought increasingly difficult. "I—yes," she managed, gripping the edge of the pianoforte for stability as the room seemed to tilt.

"Good girl," he praised, the words sending an unexpected thrill through her. His fingers found the bow of her right garter, tugging it loose with deliberate slowness. "French silk," he observed, caressing the stocking. "A secret indulgence beneath your proper exterior."

"Mother believes quality undergarments reflect a lady's true breeding," Cecilia replied absurdly, as if discussing fashion at a tea party rather than sitting half-undressed on a pianoforte with a duke between her legs.

Sebastian laughed, a warm, genuine sound that somehow made the situation less frightening and more intimate. "Your mother and I finally find something upon which to agree." His fingers rolled the first stocking down her leg with excruciating care, his touch leaving trails of fire on her skin. "Though I suspect we would disagree on the proper way to appreciate such quality."

When both stockings had been removed and discarded, he returned his attention to her petticoats, gathering the voluminous fabric and pushing it upward to reveal her final layer of defense—frilled pantalettes tied at the waist and knees with satin ribbons.

"Another engineering marvel," Sebastian observed, his fingers toying with the ribbon at her right knee. "The fortress of feminine virtue, designed by committees of grandmothers to thwart even the most determined seducer."

"You seem undeterred by the challenge," Cecilia noted, her voice embarrassingly breathless.

"I've always enjoyed a good puzzle." With a wicked smile, he untied first one knee ribbon, then the other, allowing the fabric to fall open and expose her legs fully. "Though some barriers," he added, his hands sliding up to the ribbon securing the pantalettes at her waist, "are more rewarding to overcome than others."

As his fingers worked at the bow, a sudden loud chord erupted from the pianoforte, startling them both. Cecilia had inadvertently struck several keys with her elbow, the discordant noise shattering the intimate atmosphere.

"Good heavens!" she gasped, dissolving into nervous giggles. "I believe the pianoforte objects to our misuse of its person."

Sebastian's laughter joined hers, his forehead dropping to rest against her shoulder as his body shook with mirth. "Perhaps it's offering musical accompaniment to our dance."

When their laughter subsided, he raised his head, his expression turning serious as he cupped her face in his hands. "We can stop here, if you wish," he said, his voice gentle despite the obvious desire darkening his eyes. "There would be no shame in it."

The offer—giving her control when he could easily have pressed his advantage—cemented her decision. "I don't wish to stop," Cecilia said firmly, reaching for the ribbon herself. "Though perhaps the pianoforte isn't the most appropriate venue for the conclusion of our dance."

"An excellent point." Sebastian helped her down, keeping her steady as her bare feet touched the cool floor. "There's a chaise by the window that might better serve our purposes."

He led her to the velvet-upholstered chaise, but before she could sit, he captured her in another kiss, this one slower and deeper than before. His hands moved to the thin straps of her chemise, easing them down her shoulders until the garment slipped to her waist, exposing her breasts to moonlight and his hungry gaze.

"Perfect," he breathed, cupping their weight in his palms. "Exactly as I imagined."

"You've imagined this?" Cecilia asked, fighting the urge to cover herself.

"From the moment I saw you in the library." His thumbs brushed over her nipples, drawing them into tight peaks. "Though reality far exceeds my imagination."

When he lowered his head to capture one sensitive peak between his lips, Cecilia nearly collapsed, the sensation so intense it bordered on overwhelming. Her hands flew to his hair, whether to push him away or hold him closer, she couldn't decide.

"Oh!" she gasped as his tongue circled the hardened bud before sucking gently. "That's—I didn't know—"

"Another advantage of an experienced dance partner," Sebastian murmured against her skin, moving to lavish equal attention on her other breast. "Knowing exactly where to touch to create the most pleasurable sensations."

His mouth continued its delicious torment while his hands made quick work of the ribbon at her waist, allowing her pantalettes to fall to the floor and join her chemise, leaving her completely naked save for the loose petticoats still bunched around her waist. Before she could process her near-nudity, his hand slid between her thighs, finding the most intimate part of her with unerring accuracy.

"Already so wet," he observed with male satisfaction as his fingers explored her folds. "Your body speaks a truth your proper upbringing would deny."

Cecilia might have been embarrassed if the sensation of his touch hadn't short-circuited her capacity for shame. When one long finger slipped inside her, she bucked against his hand, a startled cry escaping her lips.

"Shhh," Sebastian cautioned, his free hand covering her mouth gently. "Unless you wish to announce our activities to the entire ball."

Cecilia nodded her understanding, and he removed his hand, replacing it with his mouth in a kiss that swallowed her moans as his fingers continued their intimate exploration. When his thumb found a spot that sent lightning through her veins, her knees finally gave way, forcing him to catch her against his chest.

"Perhaps it's time for you to lie down," he suggested, his voice strained with restraint as he guided her to recline on the chaise.

The sight of her own body—almost completely exposed, laid out for his pleasure—should have horrified her. Instead, the naked hunger in Sebastian's eyes as he looked at her made Cecilia feel powerful and desirable in a way she'd never experienced.

"You remain overdressed, Your Grace," she observed, finding courage in his obvious desire.

"A situation easily remedied." He removed his shirt in one fluid movement, revealing a torso sculpted with muscle and dusted with dark hair that narrowed to a tantalizing trail disappearing beneath his waistband.

Good heavens, Cecilia thought, her mouth suddenly dry. *No one mentioned gentlemen could look like this beneath their clothing.*

As if reading her thoughts, Sebastian smiled wickedly. "The advantages of fencing and boxing rather than simply discussing politics in gentlemen's clubs." His hands moved to the falls of his breeches, unfastening them with practiced ease. "Though I should warn you, the next part of our dance might initially cause some discomfort."

The warning barely registered as he pushed his breeches and smallclothes down his hips, revealing his fully aroused state. Cecilia's eyes widened at the sight of his erection, jutting proudly from a nest of dark curls. Its size and obvious firmness triggered a momentary panic.

That cannot possibly fit where I think it's meant to go, she thought wildly, instinctively pressing her thighs together.

Sebastian noticed her reaction and slowed his approach, kneeling beside the chaise rather than covering her body with his own. "We'll proceed at your pace," he promised, his hand returning to the apex of her thighs, gently coaxing them apart again. "Your body is designed for pleasure, Cecilia. Trust me to show you."

His fingers resumed their intimate exploration, and despite her momentary fear, Cecilia found herself responding to his touch, her hips rising to meet his hand as tension coiled tighter in her core. When he slipped first one finger inside her, then a second, stretching her gently, the initial discomfort quickly gave way to a building pressure that had her clutching at the velvet upholstery.

"That's it," Sebastian encouraged, his voice rough with restraint as his fingers found a rhythm that had her panting. "Let yourself feel everything."

The tension built to an unbearable peak, and just when Cecilia thought she might shatter from it, Sebastian curved his fingers inside her while pressing his thumb against that exquisitely sensitive spot at the apex of her folds. The world exploded into fragments of sensation, waves of pleasure radiating outward from her core as she bit her lip to stifle her cries.

"Beautiful," Sebastian murmured, watching her face as she rode out the aftershocks of her first climax. "But only the beginning."

Before she could fully recover, he moved between her thighs, positioning himself at her entrance. The blunt pressure of his arousal against her sensitized flesh drew a gasp from her lips.

"Look at me, Cecilia," he commanded softly, waiting until her eyes focused on his. "This will hurt, but only briefly. I need you to relax and trust me."

She nodded, her hands finding purchase on his shoulders as he began to push forward with exquisite care. The stretching sensation was uncomfortable but not painful, her body's natural moisture easing his entry until he encountered the barrier of her innocence.

"Breathe," he instructed, brushing a kiss across her forehead. "And forgive me for this."

With one decisive thrust, he breached the barrier, swallowing her cry of pain with a deep kiss. He remained perfectly still inside her, allowing her body to adjust to the intrusion while his lips and hands distracted her from the discomfort.

"The worst is over," he promised when he finally broke the kiss. "Now we discover the pleasure."

True to his word, the initial pain faded rapidly as Sebastian began to move within her, each careful thrust sending new sensations cascading through her body. What had seemed impossible moments ago now felt inevitable, her body accepting him completely as ancient instinct took over.

"That's it," he encouraged as her hips began to move in counterpoint to his. "Dance with me, Cecilia."

The rhythm between them built slowly, Sebastian clearly restraining himself to allow her pleasure to build again. When her breathing quickened and her inner muscles began to flutter around him, he increased his pace, driving deeper as one hand slipped between their bodies to the place where they were joined.

"Once more for me," he urged, his thumb finding that magical spot that had undone her before. "Come apart while I'm inside you."

The combination of his words, his touch, and the increasingly powerful thrusts of his body into hers pushed Cecilia over the edge a second time, this climax even more intense than the first. As she clenched around him, Sebastian's control finally snapped. His rhythm faltered, his thrusts becoming urgent and deep before he suddenly withdrew, spilling his release on her stomach with a muffled groan.

For several moments, the only sound in the music room was their ragged breathing as Sebastian collapsed beside her on the chaise, somehow managing to wedge his large frame next to her without sending them both to the floor.

"Well," Cecilia finally managed, staring at the ceiling in dazed wonder. "That was certainly educational."

Sebastian's laugh vibrated against her side. "High praise indeed for your dance instructor." He pressed a kiss to her temple, surprisingly tender after such carnal knowledge. "Though I should warn you, that was merely the basic steps. The advanced curriculum is substantially more... comprehensive."

Before Cecilia could respond, the unmistakable voice of Lady Melbourne drifted through the door from the corridor outside.

"I'm quite certain I heard the pianoforte, Thornton. Please check the music room. Those Bennington twins are forever sneaking away from the ballroom."

Sebastian sprang into action with impressive speed for a man who moments ago had appeared thoroughly spent. "Quickly," he hissed, helping Cecilia to her feet and reaching for her discarded clothing. "Your petticoats first."

What followed was the least dignified dressing scene in the history of aristocratic attire. Cecilia hopped frantically on one foot while attempting to step into her pantalettes, nearly braining herself on the corner of the pianoforte in the process. Sebastian, meanwhile, had managed to don his breeches but was battling with the turned-out sleeves of his shirt.

"My corset!" Cecilia whispered urgently, spotting it beneath the bench. "I can't possibly lace it myself!"

"No time," Sebastian replied, shoving it unceremoniously behind a curtain. "You'll have to make do without it."

"Without a corset?" Cecilia was scandalized. "That's like appearing without my skin!"

"Better undercorseted than discovered half-naked with a duke," he countered logically, helping her pull her ball gown over her head. The midnight silk settled with a whisper, but without her corset, the bodice gaped alarmingly.

"Turn around," Sebastian ordered, attempting to fasten the buttons up her back. "Damnation, these are impossible!"

"They're not designed to be fastened in haste by fumbling masculine fingers," Cecilia hissed, trying to hold the bodice closed.

A knock at the door froze them both in place.

"One moment!" Sebastian called, pitching his voice higher in a surprisingly decent imitation of a woman. To Cecilia, he whispered, "Your mask, quickly!"

She grabbed her mask from the side table, securing it with shaking hands as Sebastian made a valiant final effort with her buttons before giving up and grabbing his own mask. With no time to properly tie his cravat, he simply wound it around his neck in a casual style that somehow managed to look deliberately fashionable rather than hastily assembled.

"The window," Cecilia whispered desperately, clutching her gaping bodice closed with one hand. "Can we escape that way?"

Sebastian glanced outside. "Unless you fancy a twenty-foot drop into Lady Melbourne's prized rosebushes, I think not." He grimaced, then his expression suddenly brightened. "The pianoforte! Quickly!"

Understanding dawned as he ushered her to the instrument, lifting the keyboard cover and positioning her hands on the keys. He had barely enough time to perch beside her on the bench, adopting a pose of musical instruction, before the door opened to reveal Lady Melbourne's butler.

"Ah, Thornton!" Sebastian greeted him with aristocratic nonchalance while subtly shifting to block the butler's view of Cecilia's wardrobe malfunction. "Lady Cecilia was kind enough to demonstrate a new continental melody I encountered in Vienna. Please convey our apologies to Lady Melbourne if the music disturbed the ball."

Thornton's impassive face betrayed not the slightest reaction to finding a duke and a debutante alone in the music room, though his gaze lingered momentarily on Sebastian's improperly tied cravat. "Very good, Your Grace. Shall I inform Lady Featherington of her daughter's whereabouts? I believe she has been inquiring after Lady Cecilia."

"That won't be necessary," Cecilia interjected quickly, keeping her back firmly turned. "We're just concluding our... musical interlude and will return to the ballroom directly."

"As you wish, my lady." Thornton bowed and retreated, closing the door behind him.

The moment he was gone, Cecilia sagged against the pianoforte, accidentally striking several dissonant notes with her elbow. "Do you think he suspected?"

"Thornton has been butlering for the quality for thirty years," Sebastian replied wryly. "He has undoubtedly discovered far more compromising situations than ours. Now, let's see about making you presentable."

With more care than haste now, he managed to secure enough buttons to make her appearance passable, though without her corset, the gown fit improperly. "We'll need to retrieve your mother's shawl," he decided, assessing her critically. "And pray she doesn't notice the absence of your architectural underpinnings."

Cecilia giggled despite the precariousness of their situation. "Mother is likely too occupied with matching me to Lord Thistlewhite to notice my structural deficiencies." Her smile faded as reality reasserted itself. "Good heavens, Thistlewhite! I sent him for punch nearly an hour ago. The poor man is probably still searching for me, punch cup in hand."

Sebastian's expression darkened momentarily at the mention of her suitor. "Let him search. Perhaps the exercise will improve his conversation beyond root vegetables." He tipped her chin up, studying her flushed face with an intensity that made her breath catch. "When can I see you again? Properly, without rushed encounters and interruptions?"

The question, so direct and urgent, caught Cecilia off guard. This was supposed to be a single indiscretion, a moment of madness before she inevitably succumbed to her mother's matrimonial plans. The fact that Sebastian was already planning their next assignation suggested something beyond the casual dalliance she had anticipated.

"I... that is to say... is that wise?" she stammered, suddenly shy despite the intimacy they had just shared.

"Wise? Certainly not." His thumb traced her lower lip, still swollen from his kisses. "Necessary? Absolutely. I find myself unexpectedly captivated, Lady Cecilia Featherington. One dance lesson will not suffice."

Before she could formulate a response, he kissed her again, briefly but with a passion that left no doubt as to his sincerity. "Lord and Lady Hartwick's strawberry picnic," he said when he pulled away. "Three days hence. The estate has a remarkable orangery that is rarely visited during outdoor festivities."

Chapter 2

"The strawberry picnic," Cecilia echoed, knowing she should refuse but finding herself nodding agreement instead. "I shall develop a sudden interest in exotic citrus cultivation."

Sebastian laughed, the sound warming her from within. "An excellent cover story. Now, I'll return to the ballroom first. Wait five minutes, then follow. With any luck, no one will connect our absences."

With a final kiss that held surprising tenderness, he straightened his clothing, ran a hand through his disheveled hair, and slipped from the room, leaving Cecilia alone with her thoughts, her missing corset, and the uncomfortable realization that what had begun as a reckless adventure might be developing into something far more dangerous to her heart.

Chapter 3

Three days after Lady Melbourne's ball, Cecilia sat in her mother's drawing room, attempting to maintain an expression of polite interest as Lord Thistlewhite expounded upon his latest agricultural innovation. Her corset—firmly restored to its proper place after Betty's near apoplexy at discovering it missing from her ball attire—seemed unusually constrictive today, though whether from heightened awareness of her undergarments since her encounter with Sebastian or from the sheer boredom of Thistlewhite's monologue, she couldn't determine.

"…and by introducing the manure in February rather than March, I've increased yield by nearly twelve percent," Thistlewhite was saying, his prominent Adam's apple bobbing with enthusiasm. "My bailiff was skeptical, but the proof is in the pudding, as they say!"

"Fascinating," Lady Agatha interjected with transparent insincerity. "Isn't it fascinating, Cecilia?"

"Mmm, quite," Cecilia murmured, surreptitiously checking

the clock on the mantel. Only ten minutes had passed since tea was served, though it felt like several glacial ages.

Tomorrow is the strawberry picnic, she thought, a flutter of anticipation warming her core. *And the orangery rendezvous.* The memory of Sebastian's hands on her body made maintaining an appropriate tea-with-suitor expression increasingly difficult.

"Perhaps Lord Thistlewhite would enjoy seeing the new roses in the garden," Lady Agatha suggested with all the subtlety of a charging rhinoceros. "Cecilia, why don't you show him? The fresh air would put some color in your cheeks."

I can think of more effective methods for that, Cecilia thought wickedly, remembering how Sebastian's mouth on her breast had sent heat rushing to her face. Aloud, she said, "I fear it might rain, Mother. Perhaps another time."

Lady Agatha's eyes narrowed dangerously. "Nonsense. The sky is perfectly clear. Off you go."

Recognizing defeat, Cecilia was rising reluctantly to her feet when the butler appeared at the drawing-room door.

"The Duke of Greystone, my lady," he announced with a bow.

Lady Agatha's teacup clattered against its saucer. "The Duke of—but we're not at home!"

Too late. Sebastian strode into the drawing room as if he owned it, impeccably dressed in a bottle-green coat that emphasized the breadth of his shoulders and buff breeches that clung indecently to his muscular thighs. His cravat—which Cecilia now knew intimately could be untied in exactly four and a half counterclockwise rotations—was tied in the elaborate "Waterfall" style that had taken London by storm.

"Lady Featherington," he greeted Cecilia's mother with a bow just shallow enough to be borderline insulting. "Lady Cecilia." His eyes lingered on her for a fraction too long, a hint of a smile playing at the corners of his mouth. "Lord Thistlewhite. How unexpected to find you here. Shouldn't you be overseeing the February manuring?"

Thistlewhite turned an unfortunate shade of puce. "Your Grace," he stammered, rising to perform a bow so deep he nearly toppled into the tea tray. "An honor, truly an honor."

"To what do we owe this... unexpected pleasure, Your Grace?" Lady Agatha managed, her expression suggesting she found it about as pleasurable as an unexpected case of gout.

"I was passing by and recalled that Lady Cecilia expressed interest in a volume of poetry I mentioned at Lady Melbourne's ball." Sebastian produced a small leather-bound book from his coat pocket. "Byron's latest. Quite scandalous, but educational for a young lady of discerning literary taste."

Lady Agatha looked as though she might spontaneously combust. "How... thoughtful. Though I'm not certain Byron is entirely appropriate for—"

"Oh, but I insist." Sebastian placed the book directly into Cecilia's hands, his fingers brushing against hers with deliberate intent. "I've taken the liberty of marking several passages I found particularly... moving."

Cecilia fought to keep her expression neutral, though her cheeks betrayed her with a telling flush. "Most kind of you, Your Grace."

"Won't you join us for tea?" Lady Agatha asked with obvious reluctance, social obligation warring visibly with maternal suspicion.

"I would be delighted." Sebastian settled himself into the chair closest to Cecilia, somehow making the delicate piece of furniture seem absurdly small beneath his frame. "I do enjoy an afternoon of... stimulating conversation."

The emphasis he placed on "stimulating" sent a shiver down Cecilia's spine, memories of their encounter in the music room flashing vividly through her mind.

"Lord Thistlewhite was just sharing his agricultural innovations," Lady Agatha said desperately. "Perhaps you'd care to continue, my lord?"

"Oh, I wouldn't dream of interrupting Lord Thistlewhite's discourse on fertilizer," Sebastian replied smoothly. "Though I confess my own interests lie in less... earthy pursuits."

"Such as?" Lady Agatha prompted, clearly hoping for some gentlemanly hobby that might bore her daughter to tears.

"Art, primarily. I've recently acquired several pieces from Italy that are causing quite a stir among collectors." Sebastian accepted a cup of tea from the maid, his gaze briefly meeting Cecilia's over the rim. "The human form, executed in marble, has a particular appeal, wouldn't you agree, Lady Cecilia?"

"I have limited experience with statuary," Cecilia replied primly, though the memory of his naked form, decidedly more impressive than any marble statue, threatened to overwhelm her composure.

"A situation easily remedied. My collection is open to visitors with... appropriate appreciation for classical beauty." Sebastian turned to Lady Agatha with a smile that managed to be both charming and predatory. "Perhaps you and Lady Cecilia might tour my gallery someday, Lady Featherington? With proper chaperonage, of course."

Lady Agatha looked as though she'd rather tour the sewers of London. "How generous. Though our schedule is quite full with the Season's obligations."

"Speaking of which," Lord Thistlewhite interjected, clearly desperate to rejoin the conversation, "will you be attending

Lord Hartwick's strawberry picnic tomorrow, Your Grace?"

"Wild horses couldn't keep me away," Sebastian replied, his eyes meeting Cecilia's briefly. "I have a particular fascination with… exotic fruits."

Cecilia choked on her tea, triggering a coughing fit that required Lord Thistlewhite to pat her awkwardly on the back while Lady Agatha fanned her vigorously with a decorative ostrich feather fan.

"Perhaps some water?" Sebastian suggested, rising with apparent concern. Instead of ringing for the maid, he moved to the sideboard himself, pouring a glass of water and bringing it directly to Cecilia. As he handed it to her, he leaned close enough to whisper, "Tomorrow, one o'clock, orangery," before straightening with an expression of innocent solicitude.

"Thank you," Cecilia managed, sipping the water while avoiding her mother's suspicious gaze.

"Your Grace," Lady Agatha said with forced brightness, clearly determined to regain control of the situation, "I understand your estates in Derbyshire are quite extensive. Lord Thistlewhite's property borders our country home in Hampshire. The proximity would make visiting between families so convenient once—" She stopped abruptly, realizing she'd nearly announced a betrothal that didn't yet exist.

Sebastian's expression hardened momentarily. "How fortunate for Lord Thistlewhite to have such amiable neighbors." His tone suggested he found it anything but fortunate. "Though I've always found that absence makes encounters more… anticipated, when they do occur."

The tension in the room thickened perceptibly. Lord Thistlewhite shifted uncomfortably in his chair, clearly sensing undercurrents he didn't understand. Lady Agatha's fan moved with increasing agitation, stirring the elaborate arrangement of feathers adorning her turban until they appeared to be attempting escape.

"More tea, Your Grace?" Cecilia offered, desperate to break the awkward silence.

"Thank you, no." Sebastian's easy smile returned. "Though perhaps we might continue our discussion of Byron's poetry? The passage I marked on page forty-three is particularly relevant to our... mutual interests."

Before Cecilia could respond, Lady Agatha snatched the book from the side table where Cecilia had placed it. "I shall review it first, to ensure its suitability," she announced, tucking it into her reticule with the air of a customs officer confiscating contraband.

"By all means," Sebastian replied with a smile that suggested he found her maternal vigilance amusing rather than deterring. "Though I should warn you, some passages may cause palpitations in those of... delicate sensibilities."

Lady Agatha's nostrils flared with indignation. "I assure you, Your Grace, my sensibilities are perfectly robust."

"Excellent. Then you'll particularly enjoy the poem on page sixty-seven. A rather vivid description of a sultan's harem that had the censors in absolute fits." Sebastian sat back, sipping his tea with an expression of perfect innocence that Cecilia now recognized as highly dangerous.

Lord Thistlewhite, desperate to reassert his presence, cleared his throat loudly. "Lady Cecilia, I've composed a new verse comparing your eyes to—"

"Speaking of composition," Sebastian interrupted smoothly, "I understand Lady Cecilia plays the pianoforte quite skillfully. Perhaps you might favor us with a demonstration?"

Cecilia nearly dropped her teacup. "I fear I'm rather out of practice, Your Grace." *And the last time I encountered a pianoforte in your presence, it was supporting activities decidedly unrelated to music,* she added silently.

"Nonsense! Cecilia practices daily," Lady Agatha insisted, clearly eager for any activity that might showcase her daughter's accomplishments to Lord Thistlewhite. "The pianoforte in the morning room is newly tuned. Perhaps you gentlemen would care to accompany us?"

"I can think of nothing more delightful," Sebastian replied, rising and offering his arm to Cecilia before Lord Thistlewhite could react. "If I may escort the performer?"

With no socially acceptable way to refuse, Cecilia placed her hand on his arm, hyperaware of the solid muscle beneath the fine wool of his coat. As they followed Lady Agatha from the room, Lord Thistlewhite trailing dejectedly behind, Sebastian leaned slightly closer.

"Your mother seems determined to pair you with Turnip Lord," he murmured, his voice pitched for her ears alone. "Should I be concerned?"

The question, casual as it seemed, carried surprising weight. "My mother has been determining my future since birth," Cecilia replied quietly. "Her success rate is questionable at best."

Sebastian's laugh, quickly disguised as a cough, earned a suspicious glance from Lady Agatha as they entered the morning room. The pianoforte stood by the window, sunlight gleaming on its polished surface—a far cry from the moonlit instrument that had witnessed their passionate encounter.

"Perhaps 'The Harmonious Blacksmith'?" Lady Agatha suggested as Cecilia took her seat at the keyboard. "Lord Thistlewhite is particularly fond of Handel."

Chapter 3

"Actually," Sebastian interjected, moving to stand beside the pianoforte, effectively blocking Lord Thistlewhite's view, "I'd be fascinated to hear the continental piece Lady Cecilia was practicing at Lady Melbourne's. Something about the... fingering technique was quite revolutionary."

Cecilia's hands froze above the keys as heat flooded her face. "I'm afraid I don't recall it well enough to perform," she managed, shooting him a warning glance.

"Allow me to refresh your memory." Before anyone could object, Sebastian seated himself beside her on the bench, their thighs pressed together in a manner that sent her pulse racing. "I believe it began something like this."

He placed his hands on the keyboard, surprisingly skilled fingers coaxing a melody that Cecilia vaguely recognized as a Viennese waltz. What her mother and Lord Thistlewhite couldn't see was his other hand, which had slipped beneath the bench to rest casually on her knee, his thumb tracing small circles through the fabric of her gown.

"Perhaps Lady Cecilia would like to join me?" Sebastian suggested, his expression perfectly innocent while his hand inched slightly higher on her thigh.

Swallowing hard, Cecilia placed her trembling hands on the keyboard, attempting to follow his lead while maintaining her composure despite his wandering touch. The result was a somewhat discordant duet, her timing thrown off each time his fingers traced a particularly sensitive spot.

"Charming," Lady Agatha pronounced with a forced smile after they concluded the piece. "Though perhaps a bit too... continental for English drawing rooms. Lord Thistlewhite, I believe you mentioned an interest in Cecilia's watercolors? They're displayed in the gallery upstairs."

43

Lord Thistlewhite, who had been watching the pianoforte duet with increasing dismay, seized the opportunity eagerly. "I would be most gratified to view Lady Cecilia's artistic endeavors!"

"Excellent!" Lady Agatha rose with obvious relief. "Your Grace, it has been most... unexpected to receive you today, but I fear we have another appointment shortly."

"Of course." Sebastian stood, executing a bow of impeccable correctness that nonetheless managed to convey subtle mockery. "I wouldn't dream of imposing further. Though perhaps before I depart, Lady Cecilia might show me the rose garden I've heard so much about? I'm considering redesigning the beds at Greystone Hall and would value her opinion on varieties."

Lady Agatha's expression suggested she'd rather introduce her daughter to a den of vipers than allow her alone in a garden with the Duke. "I fear the gardener is applying new fertilizer today. The aroma would be most unpleasant."

"How unfortunate." Sebastian didn't appear remotely disappointed. "Another time, perhaps. Lady Cecilia, may I have a moment to discuss one particular passage in Byron before I depart? I believe it might answer a question you posed at Lady Melbourne's regarding... poetic structure."

Before Lady Agatha could object, Sebastian had drawn Cecilia slightly aside, positioning them near the window where the heavy damask curtains partially shielded them from view. He made a show of opening a different book he produced from his pocket, pointing to a page while murmuring, "One o'clock tomorrow. Wear something easy to remove."

"You're incorrigible," Cecilia whispered back, maintaining a façade of literary interest. "My mother is watching us like a hawk stalking a field mouse."

"Your mother underestimates both my determination and your resourcefulness." His fingers brushed hers as he turned a page. "I haven't been able to think of anything but you since our dance lesson."

The admission, delivered in that same low, intimate tone, caused a flutter in Cecilia's stomach that had nothing to do with fear of discovery. "Nor I you," she confessed, surprising herself with her honesty.

Sebastian's eyes darkened momentarily with something that went beyond mere desire. "Tomorrow, then. Wear the blue gown—the one from Lady Melbourne's. I've had dreams about removing it again, this time without interruption."

Before Cecilia could respond, Lady Agatha swooped down upon them like an avenging angel in excessive plumage. "Your Grace, how illuminating this visit has been, but I fear we must prepare for our next engagement."

"Of course." Sebastian closed the book with a snap, his public persona sliding seamlessly back into place. "Lady Featherington, Lady Cecilia, Lord Thistlewhite—a pleasure, as always." His bow encompassed all three, though his eyes remained fixed on Cecilia. "Until our next meeting."

As the butler escorted him out, Lady Agatha rounded on Cecilia with narrowed eyes. "What was that about?"

"Poetry, Mother," Cecilia replied with wide-eyed innocence. "The Duke has surprisingly literary tastes."

"Hmph." Lady Agatha clearly didn't believe a word. "I forbid you to accept any more books from that man. His reputation with women is positively scandalous."

"Is it?" Cecilia asked, affecting ignorance while inwardly cataloging exactly how well-earned that reputation was. "How fascinating."

"It is not fascinating, it is appalling," Lady Agatha snapped. "Lord Thistlewhite, on the other hand, represents everything desirable in a potential husband—stability, proximity, and a complete lack of scandal."

And turnips, Cecilia added silently. *Don't forget the turnips.*

"Now," Lady Agatha continued, taking Lord Thistlewhite's arm with determined cheerfulness, "let us view those watercolors, and perhaps afterward, Cecilia can serve us some of Cook's excellent tea cakes in the garden. The one furthest from where the gardener is working," she added with a pointed glare at her daughter.

As she followed her mother and Lord Thistlewhite from the room, Cecilia's thoughts were already on tomorrow's strawberry picnic and the orangery assignation. The blue gown was currently being spot-cleaned after an unfortunate encounter with Lady Jersey's punch cup, but her green muslin had nearly as many conveniently located buttons.

One o'clock, she thought, a smile tugging at her lips despite Lord Thistlewhite's droning commentary on her admittedly mediocre watercolor technique. *I shall develop a sudden, passionate interest in citrus cultivation approximately ten minutes before.*

Chapter 4

Lady Hartwick's annual strawberry picnic was the social event of mid-Season, eagerly anticipated by the ton for its spectacular gardens, exceptional strawberries, and opportunities for genteel flirtation among the shrubbery. The weather had obliged with sunshine and gentle breezes, allowing ladies to display their finest summer gowns without fear of sudden downpours.

Cecilia, having convinced Betty that her green muslin with its twenty-seven pearl buttons was the only acceptable choice for the occasion, found herself seated beneath a striped pavilion, feigning interest in a lively debate between her mother and the Countess of Wexford regarding the appropriate number of feathers permissible in a turban before it might be considered "excessively ostentatious."

"More than seven is simply vulgar," Lady Agatha pronounced with the certainty of one who currently sported exactly seven ostrich plumes in her headdress. "Though exceptions might be made for particularly small feathers if arranged with suitable restraint."

The Countess, whose turban featured what appeared to be an entire peacock's worth of plumage, sniffed disapprovingly. "Fashion has moved beyond such arbitrary limitations, Lady Featherington. The Princess of Wales herself wore twelve feathers at her last appearance."

"Yes, well." Lady Agatha's tone suggested that even royalty could occasionally lapse into questionable taste. "The Princess has always been rather… continental in her sensibilities."

Cecilia surreptitiously checked the small enameled watch pinned to her spencer. Twelve forty-five. Fifteen minutes until her scheduled rendezvous with Sebastian. Her stomach performed a complicated acrobatic routine at the thought.

"Lady Cecilia!" Lord Thistlewhite materialized beside her chair, his gangly frame casting a shadow across her lap. "I've been searching for you everywhere! The strawberries are at their peak of ripeness. Might I escort you to the refreshment pavilion?"

Drat and double drat, Cecilia thought, manufacturing a regretful smile. "How thoughtful, Lord Thistlewhite, but I've promised Lady Hartwick I would visit her orangery at one o'clock. She's propagating a rare species from the West Indies that flowers only once a decade."

"The orangery?" Lord Thistlewhite's face fell visibly. "But the strawberries—"

"Will undoubtedly remain delicious upon my return," Cecilia finished smoothly, rising from her chair with determined grace. "Mother, you'll excuse me? Lady Hartwick was most insistent that I view her citruses at their peak perfection."

Lady Agatha, still engrossed in the feather debate, waved a dismissive hand. "Of course, dear. Though do return promptly. Lord Thistlewhite has expressed interest in walking through the rose garden with you afterward."

"How lovely," Cecilia replied with a smile that made her cheeks ache. "I shall look forward to it immensely."

Like one anticipates a tooth extraction, she added silently, gathering her reticule and parasol.

Lord Thistlewhite, displaying unexpected persistence, fell into step beside her. "Perhaps I might accompany you to the orangery? I maintain a small collection of exotic plants myself, you know. Nothing so grand as Lady Hartwick's, of course, but my gardener has had remarkable success with lemons."

Cecilia's carefully laid plans threatened to collapse around her. "How... fascinating. Though I believe Lady Hartwick mentioned the heat and humidity might be uncomfortable for gentlemen in formal attire. The tropical conditions, you understand."

"Oh!" Lord Thistlewhite tugged at his excessively starched collar, which already showed signs of wilting in the summer warmth. "Yes, I see. Most considerate of you to warn me. Perhaps I shall await your return by the strawberry pavilion, then."

"Excellent idea." Cecilia rewarded him with her most dazzling smile, which seemed to render him momentarily stunned. Taking advantage of his dazed state, she quickly added, "Don't wait if I'm delayed, though. Lady Hartwick can be quite thorough in her botanical explanations."

Before he could recover enough to reply, Cecilia hurried away along the gravel path that led toward the far end of the gardens where the orangery stood, a magnificent glass structure gleaming in the afternoon sun. Her heart raced with a combination of anticipation and trepidation—not fear of discovery, precisely, but of her own increasingly powerful response to Sebastian.

This is becoming dangerous, she admitted to herself, navigating a particularly picturesque arrangement of shrubs with practiced grace. *This was supposed to be a single indiscretion, not a series of increasingly risky assignations.*

Yet she couldn't deny the thrill that coursed through her at the thought of seeing him again, of feeling his hands on her body, his mouth against hers. It was a hunger she'd never experienced before meeting him—one that propriety insisted she shouldn't feel at all, yet seemed as natural as breathing.

The orangery loomed ahead, its glass panes refracting sunlight into rainbow patterns on the gravel path. Cecilia glanced over her shoulder to ensure she wasn't observed, then slipped through the ornate iron door into a world of warmth, moisture, and exotic scents.

The interior was a jungle of tropical plants arranged in artful groupings. Massive orange and lemon trees heavy with fruit lined the central aisle, while more exotic specimens from far-flung corners of the Empire created green walls that divided the space into private alcoves. The air was thick with humidity and the heady perfume of citrus blossoms.

"Lady Hartwick's pride and joy," Sebastian's voice came from behind a magnificent banana plant, its massive leaves creating a natural screen. "Though I suspect you're not here for horticultural education."

He stepped into view, and Cecilia's breath caught. He wore informal country attire—buckskin breeches, a loose-fitting shirt open at the throat, and a waistcoat in a shade of blue that matched his eyes perfectly. Without his formal coat and elaborately tied cravat, he appeared younger, more approachable, and somehow even more dangerously attractive.

"The green muslin," he observed, his gaze traveling appreciatively over her form. "Not the blue as requested, but I find I don't mind the substitution. The color suits your eyes."

"The blue suffered an unfortunate collision with Lady Jersey's punch cup," Cecilia explained, suddenly shy despite their previous intimacies. "Betty is still attempting to remove the stain."

"A tragedy for the gown, but perhaps fortuitous for us." Sebastian moved closer, reaching for her hand and raising it to his lips. "This one appears to have even more buttons than its predecessor. I do enjoy a challenge."

The touch of his mouth against her knuckles sent a frisson of awareness through her body, awakening memories of where else those lips had been. "I counted twenty-seven while dressing this morning," she admitted. "Betty complained quite vigorously about their excessive number."

"Betty and I find ourselves in rare agreement." Sebastian didn't release her hand, instead using it to draw her deeper into the orangery, past towering palms and flowering vines until they reached a secluded alcove furnished with a rattan chaise and small table. "Lady Hartwick's private reading nook, where she escapes her gossiping guests to enjoy horticultural journals in peace."

"How convenient," Cecilia murmured, allowing him to guide her to the chaise. "One might almost suspect you of arranging things."

"I would love to claim such foresight, but I merely observed Lady Hartwick's habits during previous social events." Sebastian settled beside her, close enough that their thighs pressed together through layers of muslin and buckskin. "Though I have been plotting how to get you alone since that disastrous tea party."

"You were the disaster," Cecilia pointed out, though she couldn't suppress a smile at the memory of her mother's horrified expression. "Mother has forbidden me from accepting any more books from you. She's convinced Byron will corrupt my sensibilities."

"Byron is an amateur compared to what I have in mind for your sensibilities." Sebastian's hand found her waist, drawing her closer as his lips skimmed the sensitive spot beneath her ear. "I've thought of little else since our music room encounter."

"Nor I," Cecilia admitted, tilting her head to allow him better access to her neck. "Though that's hardly proper for a young lady to confess."

"I have no interest in propriety," Sebastian murmured against her skin. "Only in you."

The simple statement, delivered in that low, intimate tone, sent a shiver of something deeper than mere desire through Cecilia. Before she could examine the feeling, his mouth found hers in a kiss that obliterated coherent thought.

This kiss was different from their previous encounters—less urgent but somehow more thorough, as if he were memorizing the taste and texture of her mouth. His tongue traced the seam of her lips, seeking and gaining entry without resistance as Cecilia melted against him, her hands finding purchase on his shoulders.

When they finally broke apart, both breathing heavily, Sebastian rested his forehead against hers. "I've been attending insipid social events for a week just for the chance to see you across crowded rooms," he confessed. "I think I'm losing my mind."

The admission surprised her with its vulnerability. "I've been hiding Byron's poetry beneath my pillow," she replied with equal honesty. "The passages you marked make it difficult to sleep."

Sebastian's laugh was low and warm against her cheek. "Good. I want to haunt your dreams as you've haunted mine." His hands moved to the modest neckline of her gown, fingers tracing the edge where fabric met skin. "Now, about these twenty-seven buttons…"

He turned her gently, exposing her back to his attentions. Unlike their frantic disrobing in the music room, Sebastian took his time with each pearl button, pausing between each one to press kisses to the gradually exposing skin of her back.

"This is how it should be done," he murmured, his breath warm against her shoulder blade as another button surrendered. "Slowly, with proper appreciation for each new revelation."

By the fifteenth button, Cecilia was trembling with anticipation, each brush of his fingers and press of his lips against her spine sending sparks of pleasure throughout her body. When the final button released and her bodice gaped forward, Sebastian eased the gown down her arms, trapping them temporarily at her sides as he pressed open-mouthed kisses to the nape of her neck.

"You have the most beautiful skin," he murmured, helping her free her arms from the sleeves and allowing the gown to pool at her waist. "Like alabaster warmed by sunshine."

His hands circled her waist from behind, fingers splaying across her stays as he drew her back against his chest. Through the thin fabric of her chemise and the fine lawn of his shirt, she could feel the heat of his body, the solid strength of him a stark contrast to her own softness.

"I want to take my time with you today," Sebastian said, his voice roughened with desire as his hands slid upward to cup her breasts through her corset and chemise. "No rushing, no interruptions. Just hours of pleasure until you can't remember your own name, much less propriety."

The promise in his words sent liquid heat pooling between Cecilia's thighs. "We have only until three o'clock," she reminded him breathlessly as his thumbs circled her nipples through the fabric. "Mother expects me to walk with Lord Thistlewhite through the rose garden."

Sebastian's hands stilled momentarily. "Thistlewhite again," he muttered, an edge entering his voice. "Your mother seems determined to pair you with that walking collection of agricultural factoids."

"Mother believes proximity in Hampshire outweighs all other considerations in a match," Cecilia replied, turning in his arms to face him. "Including personality, intellect, and conversational ability."

"And what do you believe?" Sebastian asked, his expression suddenly serious as his hands settled on her waist.

The question caught Cecilia off guard. This was supposed to be a dalliance, a secret indulgence before she inevitably made the sort of respectable marriage her mother had planned since her birth. Sebastian wasn't supposed to care about her opinions on matrimony.

"I believe," she said slowly, choosing her words with care, "that marriage should involve more than geographical convenience and compatible family connections. That perhaps one's husband should be someone whose company doesn't make one contemplate the sweet release of death after five minutes of conversation about root vegetables."

Sebastian's laugh seemed to hold genuine relief. "A radical

position for a debutante." His fingers found the laces of her corset, beginning the now-familiar process of loosening her stays. "Though one I find myself enthusiastically supporting."

As the pressure of her corset eased, Cecilia took a deep breath, reveling in the simple pleasure of unrestricted breathing. Sebastian slid the loosened garment forward, removing it entirely and dropping it unceremoniously beside the chaise.

"Better?" he asked, his hands returning to her waist, now protected only by the thin linen of her chemise.

"Much," she agreed, her own hands growing bold as she reached for the buttons of his waistcoat. "Though you remain excessively clothed for the tropical environment."

"A situation easily remedied." He shrugged out of the waist-coat as soon as she unfastened the last button, then reached for the hem of his shirt, pulling it over his head in one fluid movement.

The sight of his bare torso in daylight rather than moonlight was even more impressive than Cecilia remembered. Broad shoulders tapered to a narrow waist, his chest dusted with dark hair that formed a tantalizing trail disappearing beneath his waistband. Without thinking, she reached out to touch him, her fingers exploring the firm muscle beneath warm skin.

Sebastian sucked in a sharp breath at her touch, capturing her hand and bringing it to his lips. "Careful," he warned, his voice strained. "I'm attempting to proceed slowly, and your explorations threaten my resolve."

"Perhaps I don't want slow," Cecilia replied, surprising herself with her boldness.

Something dangerous flashed in Sebastian's eyes. "Do you know what you're asking for?"

"No," she admitted honestly. "But I trust you to show me."

With a sound somewhere between a groan and a growl, Sebastian pulled her against him, his mouth claiming hers in a kiss that held nothing back. His hands were everywhere—tangling in her carefully arranged curls, skimming her sides, cupping her bottom to press her more firmly against the growing evidence of his desire.

When they broke apart, both breathing heavily, he made short work of her remaining garments, helping her shimmy out of her gown and petticoats until she stood before him in nothing but her thin chemise, stockings, and garters.

"Beautiful," he murmured, his gaze traveling over her with such naked hunger that Cecilia felt her skin flush with heat rather than embarrassment. "Lie back on the chaise."

She obeyed, settling against the rattan as Sebastian knelt beside her, his fingers finding the ribbon of her right garter. With deliberate slowness, he untied the bow, rolling the silk stocking down her leg with the same care one might use when handling precious artwork. When both stockings had been removed, he pressed a kiss to the inside of her ankle, then another slightly higher on her calf.

"What are you doing?" Cecilia asked, her voice catching as his mouth continued its upward journey along her leg.

"Expanding your education," Sebastian replied, his breath warm against her inner thigh as his hands urged her legs further apart. "There are pleasures beyond what we've explored thus far."

Before she could question him further, his mouth was there—on the most intimate part of her, his tongue finding and circling the sensitive bud at her center with devastating precision. Cecilia gasped, her hands flying to his hair, uncertain whether to push him away or hold him closer as sensation overwhelmed her.

"Sebastian!" she managed, the impropriety of his actions warring with the undeniable pleasure they created.

He looked up briefly, his eyes dark with desire. "Trust me," he murmured, before returning to his ministrations with renewed purpose.

And Cecilia did trust him, surrendering to the building pleasure as his tongue worked magic against her sensitive flesh. When he slid one finger inside her, then another, curling them in a come-hither motion that hit some previously undiscovered spot deep within, the tension that had been building shattered into a thousand sparkling fragments. Her back arched off the chaise as waves of pleasure radiated outward from her core, her hands clutching at the rattan beneath her.

Before she could fully recover, Sebastian rose, unfastening his breeches with urgent movements and pushing them down his hips along with his smallclothes. His erection sprang free, jutting proudly from its nest of dark curls, and this time Cecilia felt anticipation rather than fear at the sight.

"I need to be inside you," he said, his voice rough with restraint as he positioned himself between her thighs. "Tell me if I hurt you."

The initial stretch as he pushed forward was intense but not painful, her body still sensitive from her climax but welcoming him more easily than their first time. When he was fully seated within her, Sebastian paused, his forehead resting against hers as they both adjusted to the sensation.

"Alright?" he asked, pressing a surprisingly tender kiss to the corner of her mouth.

"More than alright," Cecilia assured him, her hands finding purchase on his shoulders as she experimentally shifted her hips, taking him even deeper.

Sebastian groaned, the sound rumbling through his chest and into hers where they were pressed together. "You'll be the death of me," he muttered, but began to move within her, establishing a rhythm that had her gasping with each thrust.

Unlike their first encounter, there was no rush, no fear of discovery driving their pace. Sebastian took his time, alternating between deep, penetrating thrusts and shallow movements that teased her sensitive entrance. His hands weren't idle either, skimming over her breasts, pinching her nipples lightly, then sliding between their bodies to find the spot where his earlier attentions had brought her such pleasure.

"I want to feel you come apart around me," he murmured against her ear, his fingers circling her sensitive bud in time with his thrusts. "Let go for me, Cecilia."

The combination of his words, his touch, and the increasingly powerful thrusts of his body into hers pushed her over the edge a second time, her inner muscles clenching rhythmically around him as pleasure crashed through her in waves. The sensation of her climax triggered Sebastian's release; with a final, powerful thrust, he withdrew from her body, spilling his seed on her stomach with a muffled groan of completion.

For several moments, they remained tangled together on the chaise, their breathing gradually slowing as reality reasserted itself. The distant sounds of the picnic—laughter, conversation, the occasional burst of music from the small orchestra Lady Hartwick had engaged—filtered through the dense foliage surrounding their secluded alcove.

"We should rejoin the festivities before we're missed," Cecilia said eventually, though she made no move to disentangle herself from Sebastian's embrace.

"Five more minutes," he murmured, pressing a kiss to her temple. "I'm not ready to share you with society yet."

The simple statement, coupled with the tenderness of the gesture, caused an unfamiliar tightness in Cecilia's chest. This was supposed to be a physical arrangement, an education in pleasure before she resigned herself to marriage with someone suitable. Sebastian wasn't supposed to want more than her body, and she certainly wasn't supposed to want more from him.

Yet as they lay intertwined in the humid warmth of the orangery, the scent of citrus blossoms surrounding them, Cecilia couldn't deny that something had shifted between them—something that made this considerably more complicated than the simple dalliance she'd initially agreed to.

"Lady Cecilia?" Lord Thistlewhite's voice, far too close for comfort, shattered the moment. "Are you in here? Lady Featherington sent me to escort you to the rose garden."

Sebastian tensed against her, his expression darkening. "Bloody hell," he muttered, reluctantly disentangling himself from her embrace. "Your persistent suitor has the worst timing in England."

Panic flooded Cecilia as she scrambled to gather her discarded clothing. "He can't find us like this!"

"Agreed." Sebastian was already stepping into his breeches, fastening them with practiced efficiency. "Get dressed as quickly as you can. I'll create a diversion."

"Lady Cecilia?" Lord Thistlewhite called again, his voice moving closer through the labyrinth of exotic plants. "The gardener mentioned you'd been admiring the citrus collection."

Cecilia struggled with her chemise, which had somehow become tangled in her haste. Sebastian, already half-dressed, knelt to help her, his fingers surprisingly gentle as he straightened the garment.

"Your corset," he whispered, reaching for the discarded garment. "Turn around."

With remarkable speed, he positioned the corset around her torso, lacing it loosely—not the proper tightness for public appearance, but sufficient to support her gown. "It will have to do," he muttered, helping her step into her petticoats and gown. "I can only manage about half these damned buttons. Can you reach the rest?"

"I'll have to," Cecilia whispered back, fumbling with the pearl fastenings as Sebastian pulled on his shirt and waistcoat. "Go, create your diversion before he reaches this alcove!"

Sebastian paused, pressing a swift, hard kiss to her mouth before slipping behind a massive palm plant. Moments later, Cecilia heard a crash from the far end of the orangery, followed by Sebastian's voice raised in apparent dismay.

"Good God, what a disaster! Lord Thistlewhite, is that you? Thank heavens! Help me right this pot before Lady Hartwick's prized Jamaican pineapple is completely destroyed!"

Lord Thistlewhite's footsteps hurried away from Cecilia's hiding spot, giving her precious seconds to finish dressing. Her fingers flew over the remaining buttons, managing to secure most of them before she heard Sebastian continuing his performance.

"My profound apologies, Lady Hartwick will be devastated. I was admiring the specimens and took a wrong step. Clumsy of me. Here, if you could just help me lift from that side—careful of the thorns!"

Cecilia used the distraction to quickly check her appearance in a small decorative mirror hanging nearby. Her hair was hopelessly mussed, her cheeks flushed, and several buttons near the top of her gown remained unfastened, but with her spencer draped artfully over her shoulders, she might pass casual inspection.

Taking a deep breath to compose herself, she emerged from the alcove, affecting an expression of surprise as she rounded a large orange tree to find Sebastian and Lord Thistlewhite attempting to right an enormous terracotta pot containing what appeared to be a prickly, miniature palm tree.

"Oh! What's happened?" she exclaimed, hurrying forward with appropriate feminine concern.

Lord Thistlewhite looked up, his already ruddy complexion deepening at the sight of her. "Lady Cecilia! The Duke had a small accident with Lady Hartwick's pineapple plant."

"Entirely my fault," Sebastian interjected smoothly, shooting her a warning glance that clearly communicated *stay back* as she moved to assist. "I was so engrossed in the exotic specimens I failed to watch where I was stepping. Fortunately, Lord Thistlewhite arrived in time to help minimize the damage."

"How fortunate indeed," Cecilia agreed, carefully keeping her distance from the soil-strewn area, acutely aware that her stockingless state might be noticed if she ventured too close. "Mother sent you to find me, Lord Thistlewhite?"

"Yes!" Thistlewhite straightened, brushing soil from his hands with a look of distaste. "She mentioned you'd expressed interest in walking through the rose garden before the afternoon tea is served."

"How thoughtful of her to remember," Cecilia replied, infusing her voice with an enthusiasm she didn't remotely feel. "Though perhaps I should return to the pavilion first to... freshen up." She gestured vaguely at her hair, which despite her best efforts, still bore evidence of Sebastian's passionate attentions.

"An excellent idea," Sebastian agreed, his expression perfectly bland though his eyes danced with private amusement. "The tropical environment can be quite taxing on a lady's complexion. Lord Thistlewhite, perhaps you might inform Lady Featherington that her daughter will join her shortly? I'll escort Lady Cecilia to the main path before returning to help the gardener repair my damage."

Thistlewhite hesitated, his gaze darting between them with the first stirrings of suspicion. "I'm sure Lady Cecilia can find her way unassisted, Your Grace. I'd be happy to escort her myself."

"Nonsense," Sebastian countered smoothly. "You're needed here to explain the situation to Lady Hartwick if she arrives before I return. As the one responsible for the mishap, I should be the one to face her wrath, but someone must prepare her for the shock. You have such a diplomatic way about you—much better suited to the task than myself."

The blatant flattery worked its magic on Thistlewhite, whose chest puffed visibly at the Duke's praise. "Well, when you put it that way... I suppose I could remain to explain things to Lady Hartwick."

"Excellent!" Sebastian clapped him on the shoulder, leaving a dusty handprint on his immaculate coat. "We won't be but a moment. Lady Cecilia?"

He offered his arm with impeccable correctness, maintaining the façade of casual acquaintance as they moved toward the orangery entrance. Only when they were safely hidden by a grove of lemon trees did he pull her behind a massive terracotta pot, his mouth finding hers in a brief but passionate kiss.

"That was too close," Cecilia whispered when they broke apart, though she couldn't suppress a smile. "Poor Lord Thistlewhite. Did you have to soil his coat?"

"Consider it mild retribution for his interruption," Sebastian replied, not sounding remotely repentant. "Though I suppose I should be grateful he provided sufficient warning for us to dress. Being discovered in flagrante delicto with Lady Hartwick's prized pineapple as witness would create a scandal even my title couldn't smooth over."

"Mother would expire on the spot," Cecilia agreed, attempting to tidy her hopelessly disheveled hair. "How do I look? Presentable enough for public appearance?"

Sebastian stepped back, his gaze traveling over her with the thoroughness of a man who had recently seen every inch of her naked form. "Your spencer covers the missed buttons," he observed, reaching to adjust it slightly. "Though your hair suggests activities far more strenuous than citrus appreciation. And you might want to avoid mentioning your sudden lack of stockings."

Cecilia gasped, glancing down at her stockingless ankles. "My stockings! Where—"

"Here." Sebastian produced them from his waistcoat pocket with a wicked smile. "A souvenir of our botanical education. I'll return them at the next suitable opportunity."

"You're impossible," Cecilia scolded, though without heat. "What am I supposed to tell Mother if she notices?"

"That the tropical heat necessitated their removal to prevent swooning," Sebastian suggested, tucking the silk stockings back into his pocket. "Not entirely untrue, given the activities that caused said heat."

Before Cecilia could formulate a suitably cutting response,

voices approached from the direction of the main path—a group of elderly dowagers, by the sound of their discussion about the declining quality of society events "since the Regent's influence became so pronounced."

"Go," Sebastian urged, pressing one final kiss to her lips. "Before we're discovered. The Hartwick's musicale on Thursday—can you attend?"

Cecilia nodded, already backing away. "Mother has already accepted the invitation."

"Excellent. I'll find you there." His smile held promise that sent a shiver of anticipation down her spine despite their recent activities. "Until then, Lady Cecilia."

"Until Thursday, Your Grace," she replied with formal correctness, just as the dowagers rounded the corner, finding her alone and apparently examining a particularly fine specimen of lemon tree with scholarly interest.

As she exchanged pleasantries with the elderly ladies and allowed them to escort her back to the main picnic area, Cecilia couldn't suppress a secret smile. Lord Thistlewhite and his rose garden would have to wait. She had stockings to replace, hair to rearrange, and the lingering sensation of Sebastian's touch to savor until Thursday.

Chapter 5

By the sixth week of the Season, Lady Cecilia Featherington had developed an unexpected talent for appearing in the wrong place at exactly the right time. Whether "accidentally" encountering the Duke of Greystone in deserted libraries, conveniently losing her way in garden mazes, or developing sudden interests in various architectural features that required extensive private exploration, she had elevated clandestine meetings to an art form that would have impressed even the most seasoned spies in the Foreign Office.

Lady Agatha, growing increasingly suspicious of her daughter's newfound enthusiasm for botany, architecture, and obscure literary discussions, had responded by attaching Lord Thistlewhite to Cecilia's side with the tenacity of a barnacle to a ship's hull. This arrangement might have proven effective had Thistlewhite possessed even a modicum of guile or observational skills. Unfortunately for Lady Agatha, his obsession with agricultural innovation rendered him easily distracted by discussions of crop rotation or fertilizer composition—

distractions that Sebastian exploited with ruthless efficiency.

Their encounters, initially driven by pure physical desire, had evolved into something more complex and, Cecilia admitted privately, far more dangerous to her heart. It wasn't merely the physical intimacy—though that had certainly deepened as Sebastian introduced her to pleasures she'd never imagined existed—but the conversations that followed, the laughter they shared, the growing sense that they understood each other in ways that transcended the physical.

Which made their current situation at Lady Worcester's weekend house party in Surrey all the more precarious.

"Mother has announced her intention to secure Lord Thistle-white's proposal before we return to London," Cecilia whispered urgently to Sebastian as they stood in a darkened corridor outside the library, having engineered a brief moment alone after dinner. "She's arranged for us to take a 'private' walk tomorrow morning, with her trailing a discreet twenty paces behind. I believe she intends to physically tackle him should he attempt to escape without declaring himself."

Sebastian's expression darkened, his hand tightening where it rested on her waist. "Let him try," he growled, the possessiveness in his tone sending an inappropriate thrill through her despite the seriousness of their situation. "I'll call him out before I allow him to offer for you."

"Don't be absurd," Cecilia scolded, though secretly pleased by his reaction. "Dueling is illegal, and shooting Lord Thistlewhite over his turnip-scented proposal would create the very scandal we've been attempting to avoid."

"Perhaps a scandal is exactly what we need," Sebastian mused, his fingers tracing the edge of her décolletage with maddening lightness. "Being discovered in a compromising position would force certain… alternatives."

Cecilia stepped back, narrowing her eyes at him in the dim light. "If you're suggesting we deliberately engineer our discovery to force a marriage, I should warn you that I find such manipulation almost as objectionable as Mother's matchmaking schemes."

Sebastian had the grace to look abashed. "A fair point, and well taken." He sighed, running a hand through his already disheveled hair. "But something must be done, Cecilia. This situation cannot continue indefinitely."

"Cannot it?" she asked, vulnerability creeping into her voice despite her best efforts. "I was under the impression that arrangements such as ours typically continue even after the parties involved make suitable marriages to others."

The words hung between them, revealing the fundamental uncertainty at the heart of their affair. Sebastian's expression changed, softening into something that made Cecilia's chest tighten painfully.

"Is that what you believe this is?" he asked quietly. "An arrangement that would continue while you become Lady Thistlewhite and devote your life to admiring his exceptional turnip yields?"

Put that way, the idea seemed absurd, even repulsive. "I don't know what this is," Cecilia admitted, gesturing vaguely between them. "It began as… education. An adventure before I submitted to whatever respectable marriage Mother arranged. But now—"

She broke off as voices approached from the direction of the drawing room—other guests retiring for the evening. Sebastian quickly pulled her into a shadowed alcove, his body shielding hers from view as several gentlemen passed by, discussing the merits of various hunting grounds with the exhaustive detail that such topics inspired in country landowners.

When they had passed, Sebastian didn't immediately release her, instead cupping her face in his hands with surprising tenderness. "This is no longer merely an arrangement for me," he said quietly, his usual mockery absent. "If it ever truly was. I need you to know that before you allow your mother to engineer Thistlewhite's proposal."

The sincerity in his voice, the vulnerability in his expression—these were aspects of Sebastian that Cecilia suspected few ever witnessed. Before she could respond, footsteps approached again, these with the distinctive tap-tap rhythm of Lady Agatha's favorite walking cane.

"Cecilia!" her mother's voice called, unnervingly close. "Where have you gotten to, girl? Lord Thistlewhite has expressed interest in your opinion regarding the library's organization!"

"Library organization," Sebastian muttered under his breath. "The man grows more scintillating by the hour."

Despite the tension of the moment, Cecilia had to suppress a laugh. "I must go," she whispered. "Before she rouses the entire house party to search for me."

Sebastian's grip on her waist tightened momentarily. "Meet me tonight," he urged. "After the household retires. The Blue Room in the east wing—it's supposedly haunted, so no one has been assigned to it. I'll wait for you there at midnight."

"Midnight?" Cecilia repeated, scandalized despite their numerous previous indiscretions. "In your bedchamber? That's—"

"Not my bedchamber," he corrected quickly. "A neutral location. Please, Cecilia. We need to talk properly, without fear of interruption or discovery."

The urgency in his voice, the uncharacteristic "please"—these swayed her more than any rational argument could have. "Midnight," she agreed hesitantly. "Though how I'll evade Betty's notice—"

"Complain of a headache after dinner," Sebastian suggested. "Request a sleeping draught from Lady Worcester's housekeeper. Betty will assume you're insensible until morning."

"You've given this considerable thought," Cecilia observed, impressed despite herself.

Sebastian's smile held a hint of his usual wickedness. "Planning clandestine encounters with you has become my primary occupation. Now go, before your mother summons the militia."

With a swift, stolen kiss, Cecilia slipped from the alcove and hurried down the corridor toward the increasingly irate calls of Lady Agatha. Behind her, Sebastian remained in the shadows, watching her departure with an expression that even in the dim light revealed far more than mere desire.

"Are you quite certain you don't require my attendance through the night, m'lady?" Betty fussed, tucking the blankets around Cecilia with maternal concern. "That sleeping draught from Mrs. Wilson looked powerful strong to my eye."

"I'm certain," Cecilia assured her, affecting a drowsy expression that wasn't entirely feigned—the events of the day, coupled with the anticipation of her midnight assignation, had left her genuinely exhausted. "The headache is already fading. I simply need uninterrupted rest."

Betty looked unconvinced but nodded reluctantly. "Very well. But you'll ring if you need anything at all?"

"Of course," Cecilia promised, knowing she had no intention of summoning her maid for any reason short of the house catching fire. "Good night, Betty."

After what seemed an eternity of adjusting blankets, banking the fire, and positioning the water carafe "just so" on the bedside table, Betty finally departed, leaving Cecilia alone with the gentle ticking of the mantel clock and her increasingly nervous thoughts.

Midnight. A clandestine meeting with Sebastian in an unused bedchamber. Despite their numerous intimate encounters, this felt different—more deliberate, more significant. And his words in the corridor had suggested a conversation beyond their usual banter and passion.

This is no longer merely an arrangement for me, he had said. *If it ever truly was.*

What did that mean? Cecilia had assumed from the beginning that their affair was temporary—a pleasurable diversion for him and an education for her before they both inevitably returned to the paths society had designated. Sebastian would eventually marry some suitable aristocratic bride to continue his lineage, while she would become Lady Thistlewhite or the wife of some equally respectable, thoroughly dull gentleman approved by her mother.

The thought, which she had initially accepted as inevitable, now filled her with a hollow ache. The idea of Sebastian with a proper duchess, of herself dutifully admiring Lord Thistlewhite's agricultural innovations for decades to come—it was suddenly unbearable.

When did this become so complicated? she wondered, rising from the bed to pace the small confines of her chamber. *This was supposed to be simple. Pleasure without complications. Education without attachment.*

Yet here she was, preparing to risk her reputation even

further by sneaking through the darkened corridors of Lady Worcester's country estate to meet a man who had somehow become essential to her happiness.

The clock struck half past eleven, startling Cecilia from her reverie. She would need to depart soon if she were to navigate the unfamiliar hallways and find the Blue Room without being discovered. Moving quietly to her wardrobe, she selected a simple white dressing gown to wear over her nightgown—modest enough to preserve some dignity if discovered, yet easily removed should the conversation with Sebastian take a more intimate turn.

Not that I'm planning for that, she told herself firmly, though her body's reaction to even the thought of Sebastian suggested otherwise. *This is a serious discussion about our situation. Not another assignation.*

After arranging her pillows to resemble a sleeping form—a trick she'd read in one of the gothic novels her mother forbade—Cecilia eased open her chamber door, wincing at the slight creak of the hinges. The corridor beyond lay in darkness save for a single wall sconce casting ghostly shadows on the patterned wallpaper.

Moving with the stealth of a cat burglar, Cecilia made her way toward the east wing, pausing at each corner to listen for approaching footsteps. The house creaked and settled around her, the normal noises of an old building magnified by her heightened senses and guilty conscience.

She had nearly reached her destination when a door opened unexpectedly to her left, flooding the corridor with candlelight. Cecilia pressed herself against the wall, heart pounding, as the portly figure of Lord Worcester himself emerged, wrapped in a brocade dressing gown and carrying a candlestick.

Of all the rotten luck, Cecilia thought frantically, searching for an escape route but finding none. Discovery by her host would create precisely the scandal she'd been trying to avoid.

Lord Worcester, however, turned in the opposite direction, muttering something about "midnight sustenance" and "hidden biscuit supply," before disappearing down a servant's stair that presumably led to the kitchens. Cecilia released the breath she'd been holding, offering silent thanks that Lord Worcester's midnight appetite had apparently outweighed his observational skills.

When the coast was clear, she hurried the remaining distance to the Blue Room, hesitating only briefly before tapping softly on the door. It opened immediately, revealing Sebastian in a state of casual undress that made her breath catch—shirt open at the throat, waistcoat discarded, hair tousled as if he'd been running his hands through it repeatedly.

"You came," he said, relief evident in his voice as he ushered her inside, closing and locking the door behind her. "I was beginning to think you'd changed your mind."

"I nearly became dessert for Lord Worcester," Cecilia explained, taking in the room with curious eyes. Despite its reputation for supernatural inhabitants, the Blue Room appeared perfectly ordinary, if slightly neglected—heavy damask curtains, an ornate four-poster bed, and faded blue wallpaper that presumably gave the chamber its name. Sebastian had lit several candles, casting the space in a warm, golden glow at odds with its supposedly haunted status.

"Worcester? What was he doing prowling about at this hour?" Sebastian asked, guiding her toward a small settee positioned near the fireplace, where a modest fire provided both warmth and additional light.

"Hunting for biscuits, apparently," Cecilia replied with a smile. "His midnight appetite saved me from certain discovery and social ruin."

"I shall add 'exceptional biscuit supply' to my hospitality requirements henceforth," Sebastian declared, his attempt at levity not quite masking the tension evident in his posture as he seated himself beside her, careful to maintain a respectable distance. "Though I'm not certain 'social ruin' would be the inevitable outcome of being discovered in a corridor, fully clothed, at night."

"Mother would disagree," Cecilia observed dryly. "In her view, a young lady out of her bedchamber after dark might as well be dancing naked on the dining table during dinner service."

Sebastian's laugh held a hint of genuine amusement. "Your mother's talent for hyperbole is matched only by her collection of ornithologically-enhanced headwear." His expression sobered as he reached for her hand, his thumb tracing absent patterns on her palm. "But I didn't ask you here to discuss Lady Featherington's millinery choices or Lord Worcester's biscuit obsession."

"No," Cecilia agreed softly, her pulse quickening at his touch. "I believe you mentioned something about this no longer being merely an arrangement."

Sebastian nodded, his gaze fixed on their joined hands rather than her face—an uncharacteristic display of uncertainty from a man usually overflowing with confidence. "I've been trying to determine when exactly this changed for me," he said after a moment. "When you transformed from an intriguing diversion to... something essential."

The raw honesty in his voice made Cecilia's chest tighten painfully. "And did you reach a conclusion?" she asked, her own voice barely above a whisper.

"I thought perhaps it was that first day in the hedge maze," he replied, a small smile playing at the corners of his mouth. "Or possibly during our pianoforte duet. But in truth, I think it began the moment you tilted your head to better understand that French engraving rather than fainting in horror."

Cecilia couldn't help but laugh at the memory. "A most inauspicious beginning for a grand passion."

"On the contrary," Sebastian countered, finally meeting her eyes. "It was the moment I realized you were unlike any woman I'd ever encountered—curious rather than conventional, adventurous rather than anxious, and possessed of a mind as captivating as your physical form."

"You give me too much credit," Cecilia demurred, though warmth bloomed in her chest at his words. "I was simply too surprised to remember the proper response of a scandalized lady."

"And yet here we are, six weeks later, and you continue to surprise me." His fingers tightened around hers. "Which brings me to the reason I asked you here tonight. I cannot stand by and watch Thistlewhite offer for you tomorrow. The thought of you tied to that man for the rest of your life—forced to feign interest in agricultural innovations and bear children who might inherit his unfortunate chin—it's unbearable."

Despite the seriousness of the moment, Cecilia had to bite her lip to suppress a laugh at his description. "You paint a bleak picture of my potential future."

"Because it is bleak," Sebastian insisted, his expression intensifying. "You deserve more than resignation to a life of tedium punctuated by conversations about root vegetables."

"And what alternative would you suggest?" Cecilia asked,

heart racing as she considered the possible answers to her question.

Sebastian took a deep breath, as if steeling himself. "Marry me instead."

The words hung in the air between them, simultaneously the most natural conclusion to their affair and the most shocking proposal imaginable. Cecilia stared at him, certain she had misheard.

"I... what?" she managed finally.

"Marry me," Sebastian repeated, more firmly this time. "Become my duchess. Share my life, my bed, my ridiculous collection of French erotica."

"But... but you're the Duke of Greystone," Cecilia sputtered, her mind struggling to process his offer. "You need a proper duchess. Someone with connections and a substantial dowry, not the penniless daughter of a minor baron with a mother who wears dead birds as hair accessories."

Sebastian's laugh held genuine amusement. "I have more money than I could spend in three lifetimes, connections sufficient to make even the Prince Regent tolerate my eccentricities, and absolutely no need for a 'proper' duchess. What I need is you—your wit, your curiosity, your willingness to challenge me. And," he added with a wicked smile, "your remarkable enthusiasm for improper activities in orangeries."

Despite herself, Cecilia blushed at the memory. "You can't be serious. The ton would be scandalized. Mother would likely expire on the spot."

"The ton will gossip for precisely one week before being distracted by the next scandal, and your mother would recover remarkably quickly once she processed the advantages of having a duchess for a daughter." Sebastian's expression turned serious again as he took both her hands in his. "The real question, Cecilia, is whether you could envision a life with me. Not as a clandestine lover, but as my wife, my partner, my duchess."

The question struck at the heart of what Cecilia had been avoiding acknowledging even to herself—that her feelings for Sebastian had long since transcended physical desire or rebellious adventure. The thought of a life without him, of returning to the path her mother had mapped out for her, was suddenly unimaginable.

"I could," she admitted softly, surprising herself with the certainty in her voice. "I do. But Sebastian, are you certain? Marriage is rather more permanent than an arrangement between consenting adults."

"I have never been more certain of anything," he replied without hesitation. "I love you, Cecilia Featherington. Your intelligence, your courage, your willingness to scandalize society librarians by examining French erotica with scholarly interest. I want to spend the rest of my life introducing you to new pleasures, new ideas, new experiences—preferably without Lord Thistlewhite interrupting at critical moments."

The declaration, so unexpected and yet so perfectly Sebastian—combining sincerity with humor, passion with tenderness—broke something loose within Cecilia's carefully guarded heart.

"I love you too," she confessed, the words surprisingly easy once she allowed herself to speak them. "Though I had convinced myself this could never be more than a temporary adventure."

Sebastian's smile could have illuminated the entire east wing. "So? Will you marry me, Lady Cecilia? Save yourself from a lifetime of turnip appreciation and save me from the matchmaking mamas who parade their daughters before me like prize cattle at a fair?"

Cecilia laughed, joy bubbling up within her like champagne. "When you present it as a mutual rescue mission, how could I possibly refuse? Yes, Sebastian. I will marry you."

His response was immediate and thoroughly inappropriate for a newly engaged couple—he pulled her into his arms and kissed her with a passion that left no doubt as to the depth of his feelings or his intentions for the remainder of the night. Cecilia melted against him, her hands sliding into his hair as she returned his kiss with equal fervor.

When they finally broke apart, both breathing heavily, Sebastian rested his forehead against hers. "We should announce our engagement immediately," he murmured. "Before your mother can maneuver Thistlewhite into proposing."

"Tomorrow at breakfast?" Cecilia suggested, her fingers already working on the buttons of his shirt, belying her apparent interest in practical planning. "Though perhaps we should consider how best to present the news to minimize Mother's inevitable apoplexy."

"Tomorrow," Sebastian agreed, his own hands busy with the sash of her dressing gown. "Though I believe the remainder of tonight might be better spent celebrating our engagement in a more... private manner."

"A consummation in advance of the vows?" Cecilia teased, allowing him to push the dressing gown from her shoulders. "How scandalous, Your Grace."

"You haven't seen scandalous yet, my future duchess," Sebastian promised, his voice dropping to the velvety register that never failed to send shivers down her spine. "By the time I'm finished with you tonight, you'll have material for memoirs that would make Byron blush."

"Bold claims require substantial evidence," Cecilia challenged, gasping as his mouth found the sensitive spot beneath her ear. "I believe I shall require a thorough demonstration."

"Your wish," Sebastian murmured against her skin, "is my command."

What followed was indeed worthy of memoirs, though Cecilia had no intention of committing the details to paper, preferring to keep them locked in her memory as the first night of their engagement—the beginning of a life far different from the one she had been raised to expect, but infinitely more suited to her true nature.

Morning would bring challenges—Lady Agatha's shock, society's gossip, the logistics of transforming a clandestine affair into a proper marriage—but as Cecilia lay in Sebastian's arms in the supposedly haunted Blue Room, watching dawn light creep around the edges of the heavy curtains, she couldn't bring herself to worry about any of it.

She had found something far more valuable than propriety or her mother's approval: a partner who saw her completely—her desires, her intelligence, her unconventional spirit—and loved her not despite these qualities, but because of them.

The proper Lady Cecilia Featherington might indeed be courting scandal, but for the future Duchess of Greystone, it was merely the beginning of a most improper happily ever after.

Chapter 6

The morning sun streamed through the east-facing windows of Lady Worcester's breakfast room, illuminating an unusually tense tableau. Lady Agatha Featherington, her turban listing dangerously to one side (whether from agitation or simply poor millinery engineering remained unclear), sat rigidly in her chair, alternating between fanning herself vigorously and gulping restorative sips of tea. Across from her, Lord Thistlewhite appeared to be physically shrinking, his already weak chin receding further into his cravat with each passing moment.

Between them stood Sebastian and Cecilia, hands clasped in a clear declaration of their new status, facing the assembled house party guests with matching expressions of defiant happiness.

"Married?" Lady Agatha repeated for what must have been the fourth time, her voice scaling new heights of disbelief. "Yesterday afternoon? Without my knowledge or consent?"

"A special license is a marvelous thing, Mother," Cecilia replied serenely. "And as I am of age, consent was mine to give, not yours to withhold."

The impromptu wedding had been Sebastian's idea—a logical extension, he had argued as they lay tangled together in the Blue Room's rumpled sheets, of their engagement. Why wait for banns and settlements when a special license (conveniently procured weeks earlier, revealing a level of planning that both surprised and touched Cecilia) and the local vicar could accomplish the same result without the risk of maternal interference?

"But… but…" Lady Agatha sputtered, her fan working overtime. "The preparations! The trousseau! The settlements! The—"

"All easily handled retrospectively," Sebastian interjected smoothly. "I've already dispatched messengers to my solicitors. Lady Featherington, I assure you that your daughter's position as Duchess of Greystone will be accompanied by every financial security and social advantage."

"Duchess," Lady Agatha repeated, the title appearing to penetrate her shock where rational argument had failed. Her expression underwent a remarkable transformation, outrage giving way to calculation as she processed the social implications. "My daughter, a duchess."

"Indeed," Sebastian confirmed, his thumb tracing gentle circles on Cecilia's hand where he held it. "Though I fear we've disappointed Lord Thistlewhite's agricultural aspirations."

All eyes turned to Thistlewhite, who had remained frozen in apparent shock throughout the exchange. At the direct address, he seemed to remember himself, rising awkwardly to his feet.

"C-congratulations, Your Grace," he stammered, addressing Cecilia with the title that still felt foreign to her ears. "Most unexpected, but… felicitous. Most felicitous."

"Thank you, Lord Thistlewhite," Cecilia replied graciously. "I'm certain you'll find a bride who truly appreciates your innovative approach to crop rotation."

"One hopes," he agreed dolefully, casting a last, longing glance at Cecilia before excusing himself from the breakfast room with as much dignity as his deflated demeanor allowed.

Lady Worcester, who had observed the entire scene with the gleeful attention of a confirmed gossip presented with prime material, clapped her hands in delight. "A clandestine wedding at my house party! How perfectly thrilling! We must celebrate properly—a ball, I think, to introduce the new Duchess of Greystone to society."

"Most kind," Sebastian acknowledged with a bow. "Though I fear the Duchess and I must depart for London today. Certain arrangements require our immediate attention."

"Such haste," Lady Agatha protested, finally emerging from her shock-induced stupor. "Surely a few days to properly celebrate—"

"I'm afraid His Grace is correct, Mother," Cecilia interrupted, adopting the authoritative tone she'd been practicing privately all morning. "Greystone Hall requires my immediate attention, and we have plans to tour the Italian states this summer. The arrangements cannot wait."

The casual mention of the ducal seat and Continental travel plans—strategic references suggested by Sebastian to emphasize her new status—had the intended effect on Lady Agatha, whose objections transformed into enthusiastic planning for her own visit to Greystone Hall "once you're properly settled, of course."

As the breakfast room erupted into excited chatter, with Lady Worcester already dispatching servants to spread the news throughout the house, Sebastian leaned close to whisper in Cecilia's ear.

"Well played, Duchess. Your mother appears to be adapting to the situation with remarkable speed."

"The prospect of social advancement is a powerful restorative," Cecilia murmured back. "Though I expect a lengthy lecture on filial duty once we're alone."

"A lecture you can receive as the Duchess of Greystone, immune to her matrimonial schemes forevermore," Sebastian pointed out, his hand settling possessively at the small of her back. "Was it worth scandalizing society for that freedom alone?"

Cecilia turned to face him fully, not caring that every eye in the breakfast room was upon them. "I didn't marry you to escape Mother's matchmaking," she said softly. "I married you because the thought of life without you had become unimaginable."

Sebastian's expression softened into the tender look that she now knew was reserved exclusively for her. "Even if it means enduring the ton's gossip about our hasty union?"

"Let them gossip," Cecilia replied with newfound confidence. "In a week, some other scandal will capture their attention. And in the meantime…" She leaned closer, lowering her voice to a whisper meant for his ears alone. "I believe you mentioned plans for making me the most thoroughly educated duchess in England."

Sebastian's laugh, rich with promise and affection, drew curious glances from the assembled guests. "Indeed I did, Your Grace. And I always keep my promises—particularly the indecent ones."

As Lady Agatha approached, apparently recovered enough to begin interrogating them about wedding details and future plans, Cecilia squeezed Sebastian's hand, a silent confirmation of their shared secret and the unconventional path that had led them to this moment.

The proper Lady Cecilia Featherington had indeed ceased to exist, transformed by scandal and passion into Her Grace, the Duchess of Greystone—a metamorphosis that, despite its thoroughly improper beginnings, promised a future far more satisfying than propriety could ever have provided.

About the Author

Elena is a passionate writer of historical romance, crafting stories that span everything from brooding Victorian affairs to bawdy, outlandish pirate adventures on the high seas. Whether serious or cheeky, her tales are always rich with atmosphere, irresistible tension, and scenes that turn up the heat. Her books are perfect for readers who love history served with a wink—and a good deal of steam.

When she's not writing, Elena enjoys baking elaborate pastries and wandering antique shops in search of inspiration for her next story. She has a particular fondness for old letters and vintage postcards, often imagining the secret romances they once held. Her love of history and flirtation with the sensual makes its way into everything she creates.

Printed in Dunstable, United Kingdom